# SHANNON'S TRIAL

A gripping, action-packed thriller

# PAUL BENNETT

*Nick Shannon Thriller Book 9*

Joffe Books, London
www.joffebooks.com

First published in Great Britain in 2024

Cover art by Nick Castle

ISBN: 978-1-83526-360-0

*'For evil to rule, it takes only one good man to turn his back.'*
Nick Shannon

*'Amen to that.'*
Johnny Silver

*Trial.*
Definition 1: Judgement between innocent and guilty, between good and evil.

Definition 2: A test that has to be overcome.

# CHAPTER ONE

The heavy plastic tag around my ankle was rubbing. I would have to see whether it could be adjusted at my daily report to the police station. I was on bail, thanks to my lawyer, Martin, and to DCI Palmer speaking up on my behalf. They both said I was lucky. I had fired six bullets into the assassin who had so nearly killed my wife, Cherry, while we were standing outside on our wedding day. If I had fired the remaining bullet between his eyes as I had intended, then I would be in prison by now. Martin reckoned he could stave off the trial for another year and go for a defence of diminished responsibility: that way he might get the punishment down to two years and then get the sentence to be suspended. Anything above that, and I would be in prison for the second time in my life.

I went up to the desk sergeant and he had all the paperwork ready. Creature of habit. For both of us, I suppose.

Palmer emerged with two mugs of tea, placing one on the desk sergeant's desk.

'Early, aren't we today, Shannon?' Palmer said.

He was as immaculate as ever, deep blue suit jacket stretched over his barrel chest, crisp white shirt, spotless light blue tie. He had extreme OCD and it affected everything he did. He couldn't pass a desktop of pens without lining them up parallel or at exactly ninety degrees to each other. His short hair was grey and receding at the temples. He was over the retirement age, but would be lost without the job. I had helped him to get promotion, and that was the final factor keeping him going. When he laughed, it was infectious. Pity he didn't do it more often.

'Start on a new client this morning,' I replied.

'Whereabouts?' he asked.

'Fairstead Hospital.'

'Oh, God. My manor. I'll have SOCO on standby. Maybe get an ambulance ready, too. Or a hearse.'

'That's a bit unfair,' I said.

'Just face it, Shannon, you're a corpse magnet. Wherever you are, there's a dead body popping up. What's your average? A little over one body per contract. My motto is always "Be prepared" when you're around. At least it's a hospital, so convenient for the bodies. I'd better get the wife to put all my meals straight in the bin rather than try to keep them edible.'

'Nothing in the last six months,' I protested. 'My record is good since the shooting. I'm a changed man. A shadow of my former self.'

'Time will tell,' he said. 'You, a shadow? We'll have to see.'

'Thank you for your confidence,' I said. 'It's touching. Chokes me up.'

'Sign the book,' he said, 'and be on your way. Don't let our paths cross.'

'I need to get the tag adjusted,' I said to the sergeant. 'It's rubbing — needs loosening.'

'Um,' said the sergeant, sucking air through his teeth. 'Can't do adjustments, I'm afraid. Some tech thing. I'll need to order a new one. If I pull a favour, I should be able to get a new one in two weeks, three at the longest. If I pull a favour, like I said. Anything to justify that, Shannon?'

'What do you want?' I said, with a sigh.

'It's the annual dinner for the station in a fortnight's time. We encourage outsiders. Can I put you down for two tickets?'

'How much?' I sighed again and waited for the second scam.

'To you? Fifty quid each.'

'And to anyone else?' I said.

'Fifty quid.'

'Thank you for making me feel special,' I said. 'OK, two tickets. What's included?'

'Soft drinks and a mass-catered meal of cold something with hot gravy poured over it.'

'You've sold it to me,' I said, 'especially if you can cut the gravy in slices.'

'I'll put in a special request,' said Palmer. 'For old times' sake.'

'Well,' I said. 'Must get on. Some of us have to get some work done.'

'No snide remarks, Shannon,' Palmer said, 'or the price of the tickets goes up.'

I signed the paperwork and left. Some battles you can't win. They were chuckling as I went out the door.

\* \* \*

I drove back home in the Beamer — a BMW M3 that could outpace pretty much anything on the road. I had asked the garage to take off all the M3 logos and replace them with those of a 320d to make it less tempting for the car thieves. Wolf in sheep's clothing.

Home was a wonderful converted five-storey wharf with fabulous views over the Thames. To top it all was a mixture of good, loyal friends and workmates; a business that we had expanded because of the publicity after I had killed the Home Secretary — but that's another story.

On the ground floor of the wharf, we had an office for me with space and an additional table for visits from clients or conferences, two smaller offices for admin and an informal sitting area looking out over the river with an essential proper coffee machine. The floor above that was for all of us — I'll fill you in on that in a moment — for just relaxing or eating meals together — every storey had its own kitchen and bathroom.

The floor above that was for Norman and his partner Morag. Norman was an ex-embezzler and my cellmate in Chelmsford, who bankrolled us when Shannon Investigations, fraud detectives, was just starting out. Morag was recruited from her job as PA to the Chief Constable of Mid Anglia Police Force after one of our jobs there caused a reorganisation — and the death of the Home Secretary. Did I mention that?

The next storey was occupied by Anji, aged twenty-three, graduate from Exeter in Economics and former pole dancer. Anji was as feisty as they come and gave us lessons from the present and not the past. She kept us grounded and up-to-date. And was beautiful, too.

The top floor was for me and my recent wife Cherry Walker — Cherry in personal mode and Walker in terms of work. We'd had a love-hate relationship for many years until my wife passed away. All hate departed and the space left was filled with love. Cherry was the most beautiful woman I have ever seen. Her natural skin colour was like coffee cream, a throwback to her Iranian roots. She had cheek bones that most women would die for and glossy black hair cut to shoulder length, acting as a frame over her beautiful canvas. Her eyes were black and mesmerising — you could lose yourself in them. Her credentials were that she was ex-Fraud Squad and she had contacts there who would track car registrations, search police files and so on, as favours repaying good deeds from the past. Not quite according to the rule book, but who could resist when Cherry called? Importantly, she was now eight months pregnant with our twins and I wrapped her in tissue paper and cotton wool, much to her annoyance.

There were three people on the payroll who didn't live in — Arthur, Valentine and Beryl. Arthur was my cellmate in Brixton, who taught me how to survive in prison. Not always successfully, but without Arthur I would not be the same person as I am today. He was an ex-wrestler under the name of Arthur 'Dangerous' Duggan. He was six-foot-five and looked like a bear, which was descriptive, except he was like a Teddy bear when not threatened.

Beryl was recruited from our job at a law firm where her boss was poisoned — that's the kind of people we were. Dead clients and waifs and strays. Beryl was Morag's assistant.

Our last, and most recent recruit was Valentine. Twenty-two and lower second from Warwick in Sociology, so not the best CV in the jobs market. More relevant to his past career, however, was that he was the son of the CEO of Zeus, David Shapiro. We rescued him from a life of tedium into our world of adventure, corpses included. And he was a babe magnet. Always good to have one of those in your arsenal. All in all, we covered all the angles.

Everyone was in the river room drinking coffee when I got back, and Anji was dressed and ready to leave. For clients, she toned everything down and was wearing a disguise of a black trouser suit and white blouse, and she would be ready with a pair of glasses with plain lenses in her handbag, just to make herself look studious. They would not recognise her in her preferred outfit of crop top, skater's skirt and black over-the-knee biker's leather boots. They wouldn't know what they were missing.

I needed a cup of espresso to charge the system before setting out, and Beryl pressed the necessary buttons and levers. I sat down on one of the three sofas arranged in an open square so that there was an uninterrupted view of the river.

'All ready for the start of the new working week?' I asked everyone.

'Valentine and I are a couple of days away from finishing on Silvers,' said Walker.

Silvers was an investment bank; this was our second pro-ject sorting out money-laundering protocols and checking that they were complying to the myriad of rules which were burdensome to investment banks.

'I'd love you to meet Johnny Silver,' she said. 'You would get along well with him. He has your honesty and moral values — honour and all that goes with it. He'd make a good friend. I'll let you have some details on him and his history. Fascinating. You'd love it.'

'How are you feeling? I said to her. She — and, therefore, we — had had a restless night. I had heard that scratching was one of the side effects of pregnancy, but it still caught me out.

'How do I feel?' she said. 'Like a cross between a whale and a hippopotamus. Covered in blubber and lumbering around. I have to console myself that I can work most of the time from here — Valentine is such a help.'

He blushed.

'I've got a scan tomorrow, so we might be able to be more precise with the birth date.'

'I'll come along, if today at the Fairstead goes well,' I said.

'You don't have to,' she said.

'I'd like to,' I said. 'Incredible experience to see everything in such detail. They give you a photo of the scan, too. Be good to have, if ever we might feel down. Sort of bonding starting before the birth.'

I finished my coffee, stood up and picked up my briefcase.

'OK, Anji,' I said. 'Time to go. A new adventure awaits.'

# CHAPTER TWO

The first difference between the private sector and the NHS was on our arrival. There was lots of parking at Fairstead Hospital, so you could pull in anywhere you liked rather than going round and round in circles trying to spot someone who was leaving and jump in their space.

The second difference was the building itself. It was glass and brick-faced: no stained concrete in sight. Your heart didn't sink when standing in front of it, wondering what you would encounter inside.

Third was reception. Walking through the entrance doors, you came into an area with bright lights and, fittingly, clinical spotlessness. The walls were cream and relaxing. There were sofas scattered around with coffee tables and individual table lights. Strategically placed on the tables to show their glossy covers were upmarket magazines and the morning papers — no leaflets for STD clinics or how to cope with obesity. The chances of the clients here catching such a disease or being more than a little overweight were slim. These were people like Dorian Grey who, rather than having a picture, employed servants to be obese for them.

Behind the reception desk was a pretty woman dressed in a light blue suit with a dark blouse and a red checked neckerchief that oozed efficiency. She logged us in, issued us with badges, offered us coffee and made a phone call. We went to a pair of sofas and picked up copies of *Country Life* and *Horse and Hound*. Both magazines featured properties that would enhance my lifetime experience by only spending three million or so. My lifetime experience would be enhanced by keeping out of jail and they didn't seem to cater for that.

Coffee arrived, tasting like it came from a capsule machine, and was passable for that.

'First impressions?' I said to Anji.

'Like I'd have to remortgage my three-million-pound house just to sit here with a coffee.'

'I would imagine most of the clients here — never use the word "patients", I suspect — either have private medical insurance or sufficient funds that this is no more than a drop in the ocean. Impressive place, though.'

A young woman, red-headed, tall and slim, dressed in the same uniform as the receptionist, entered the area and came up to us. She introduced herself as Christine May, PA to Alan Cooper, CEO of the business — *business*, I noticed, not *hospital*. She said that she would give us a guided tour in advance of our meeting with Cooper. Would be rude to refuse. She was too nice to say no to. She was not unattractive — damned by faint praise — but was the girl next door. She was Olivia Newton-John in *Grease* before the transformation. Her skirt was knee length and made no statement about her except she wanted not to stand out from the crowd. Her only remarkable feature, apart from her blue eyes, was heavy lip liner to make her mouth seem plumper. Maybe they didn't offer discounts for staff.

She led us along a deep-blue carpeted corridor with doors on each side.

'These are our consulting rooms,' she said. 'Many of our clients have mobility issues — that's why they are here — new hips and so on. We don't want any restrictions on their movements. Everything is about the client. Upstairs, as we will see, is mostly our administration offices. The rest are for communal services for everyone — pharmacy, for one. It contains Alan's suite. You'll be impressed by that.'

*Suite?*

After the corridor was a T-junction. She led us to the right to what was a single-storey extension. It flowed well and was hard to see it as not originally planned. Only the likes of Anji and I took in these small details. Plus the fact that the carpet changed to a mid-grey.

'We have two operating theatres, so that we can fulfil our oath of not having to wait for that hip op.'

'And,' I said, 'do you have the staffing — surgeons, anaesthetists, nurses and so on — to deliver those promises?' I asked.

'All our consultants work for the NHS primarily, but have private practice here otherwise. You get urgency and the same medical competency, but in deluxe surroundings. We have a small reserve, just in case we need overflow. Our rooms are designed to have spare capacity pre- and post-op. Let's double back.'

We went back on the corridor until we took the left side of the split.

'These are our additional clients' rooms,' Christine said.

There were sliding notices on the doors — occupied and free — and she checked and opened the door on one of them. Inside, there was a large room with a bed, a wide window opposite the bed so you could look out at the trees and manicured lawn, two tasteful armchairs covered in red velour and one of those tables that had wheels so you could slide it over the bed. There was a door on the left-hand wall. Christine opened it and revealed an en suite bathroom with a shower which had a seat inside and a complimentary basket of high-end shampoos, shower gels, moisturisers and so on. All very swish and practical. If you had to have an operation, this was the place to go to. I marked it down for Cherry if things got complicated.

Tour over, Christine took us upstairs to meet Cooper. She knocked on a door and opened it without waiting for an answer. The room was large, but not boastfully so. It was decorated in a pastel-yellow shade of white, and was bright from the décor and two large windows looking out on the front of the building and the comings and goings of the business. There were two doors alongside one wall — what more can a person reasonably want? Between the doors sat an acoustic guitar on a stand. Interesting.

Behind a large L-shaped desk, Cooper stood up to greet us. He was tall and wiry — not slim but *wiry* — with no excess fat or highly developed muscle. He probably exercised regularly, but not in a gym. He was wearing a light grey three-piece suit with a blue button-down collar with a red tie and a small gold cross pinned to his lapel. Nothing to take objection to so far. We made introductions and shook hands. He pulled out a chair for Anji and I sat next to her on one side of the pine desk.

'Do you play?' I said to Cooper, pointing to the guitar.

'I play from time to time,' he said. 'If a client is especially down, I go along with my guitar and subject them to something tuneful — maybe a classic Spanish piece to soothe them.'

'May I?' I said.

He nodded.

I walked across to the guitar. Studied it for a while. It was right for me. I picked it up and played an E-minor chord. Two fingers and striking all six strings. Maybe the easiest chord to play. It sounded bright. I switched to an A chord — three fingers and striking only five strings. More difficult. The chord resonated sweetly through the body of the sound board. Crystal clear. This was a good guitar.

'Good choice,' I said. 'I would be unworthy of such a guitar.'

'We all find what's right for us in life,' he said.

'But for some that turns out badly,' I said.

'We could talk about philosophy for a long time,' he said, 'but that's not what you are here for. How do you want to play things?'

'Tell us the details of why we are here. What exactly do you need from us?'

'We run a successful business here,' Cooper said, 'but we are full all the days. We need to expand — like a water skier, if you don't go forward, you sink. That is a costly business. We have plans drawn up for a new extension and everything ready to go, but we can't fund it by ourselves. A lot of our work comes from NHS patients and we have put a proposal to them. Back us, and we will keep a certain capacity for their patients. We take the unfulfilled load and give the patients what they can't get — and swiftly, too.'

'And in return?' I said.

'They have to fund a quarter of the cost. That's a lot of money. We're talking millions, but that's cheap compared with the cost of a new hospital. Remember the Brexit Battlebus? The sign on that said £350 million for a new hospital.'

'And?' I said.

'They want an independent view of our business — don't trust our auditors to be impartial, turning a blind eye to keep the business. They want due diligence to the nth degree. They want the best advice before they will take a decision; thus, they have chosen you. You're a red-hot property at the moment. Milk it while it lasts.'

'What's your background?' I said. 'You will be an integral part of the deal, I take it? Probably with a long-term contract as a stipulation. Anything we should be aware of?'

'Classic training at Oxford. Good degree — first. Took an MA, which further boosted my CV. Classic medical school training. Served my time. Started out on the GP route — I wanted to help people, to make a difference — and saw what was wrong with the system. It was swamped. It was always my goal to change that. So I switched direction and took up my first job in the private sector and worked myself up the ladder. Then I had a vision of what care should be. Found a business that had the same ideas. And here I am. Fulfilling a dream.'

Anji had stopped taking notes. She looked across at me. I nodded.

'I'm searching for the right word,' she said, 'but it doesn't sound like the principle of what the NHS stands for — free for anyone, regardless of means? Uncharitable? Is that what I mean?'

'You have to be pragmatic about it,' Cooper said. 'There's not enough capacity in the NHS to meet that ideal. There's no option but for private hospitals to take its share of the load and make some money at the same time. You're talking about a communist ideal in a capitalist world. I think we, and others like us, provide a deluxe solution to an unsolvable problem. I wouldn't be sitting here if I didn't think we don't make a difference.'

'A Christian approach?' I said. 'I noticed your cross pin. Some might say that's an easy cop out — let God come up with the answer.'

'We're back to philosophy,' he said. 'We could sit here for days debating the issue without coming to an answer. Are your views likely to influence your work here?'

'We always take an unbiased approach,' I said. 'Objective throughout is our mantra. That's why we are in such demand. You can trust us. Never fear.'

'Anything else before you start work?'

Anji looked at me again. I nodded again.

'I'd like to know what's behind the two doors,' she said.

Cooper gave a laugh. 'Curiosity killed the cat, you know? But you couldn't do your job without being curious. I'd expect nothing else.'

He got up and went to the door on the right and opened it. Anji and I peered inside. It was a small room with just enough space for a coffee table and two brown Chesterfield armchairs sitting opposite each other either side of the table.

'I use this space for any private discussions. My office door is always open — it's part of my policy. If I need somewhere confidential, I use this space. It is more relaxing than the barrenness of my desk.'

He closed the door and went to the other one. Opened it. This time the space was for a wet room complete with a toilet, large wash basin and a shower.

'I cycle to work,' he said. 'A journey of five miles. Sometimes when I arrive here, I need to get rid of the sweat I've generated and the dirt that seems to hang around London. I change here from my cycling gear to the formality of a suit. I'm a detail man, too, Shannon.'

'Just one more thing before we start,' I said. Anji took two short documents from her briefcase and gave them to me. I passed them across the table to Cooper. 'Our contract,' I said. 'Sign both — I've already put my signature on them — and retain one for your records.'

He read the contents and raised a pen.

'Seems expensive,' he said.

'I tend to think you get what you pay for in life,' I said.

'More philosophy,' he said, with a sigh. Nevertheless, he signed the contract. 'Time we got you working.'

* * *

Christine appeared out of nowhere as we left Cooper's office. 'We've got you one of the consulting rooms as a base,' she said. 'It's not big — intended for just one consultant and one patient — so will be a bit of a squeeze, but it's the only space we have at the moment. I'm so sorry.'

'We appreciate it,' I said, as we walked along the corridor. 'Thoughtful.'

Christine stopped at one of the doors. 'You might as well have a look in here,' she said. 'This is the pharmacy.'

We entered the room. It was mostly taken up by shelving running across two sides of a small room. Along the shelves, there were labels to indicate the different types of medication, so that it was easy to find what you were looking for.

'I notice there are no cupboards with locks on,' I said. 'Doesn't that mean that this room is a security risk? Anyone can have access, and I suppose that some of these drugs could raise a high price on the black market?'

'We trust our staff,' she said. 'The nurses are the only ones who need access — mostly for pain relief — and we vet them deeply before we take them on. Every medicine has to be checked and signed for before being dispensed. In the history of this hospital, there has never been anything going missing. The system works and that's the important point. Let's move on.'

Further along the corridor we entered a tiny room — Christine was right; it would be a bit of a squeeze. There was small L-shaped desk with one chair on one side and two chairs on the other, just in case the patient had brought along some support.

'I've booked you in with our finance director in half an hour,' Christine said. 'She'll give you the codes to enter the system and the accounts. So, shall I get you some tea or coffee while you settle in? It really would be no problem.'

'Coffee would be very welcome. The nearest you have to espresso — thick and dark.'

'The same as Nick,' Anji said, 'but diluted. I don't want to bounce off the walls this early in the day.'

'You do realise,' I said to Anji, 'that when you dilute it it's still the same amount of caffeine as mine?'

'I was feeling virtuous until you said that,' Anji said. 'Go on, Christine; I'll have the same as Nick.'

The helpful Christine left the room and Anji and I looked at each other. 'What do you think so far?' I said.

'Seems a slick operation, if you pardon the pun,' she said. 'I can tell you feel worried about the pharmacy. Having no lock or key does seem slack, but if the system works, who are we to criticise it?'

'Because no one else will. The auditors only concern themselves with financial matters. We have to look at the whole picture, as it may affect the business. It's a low priority at the moment, so let's park it till we do the final report. What about Cooper? What do you make of him?'

'The gold cross on his lapel would seem to sum him up,' Anji said. 'A goodie-goodie. Doesn't seem to have the right mindset for committing a fraud, so we should concentrate on those below him.'

'Anything else?' I said.

'Plays a guitar. The guitar-playing nun in *Airplane* could be a similarity. Forcing himself on his patients to indulge his hobby.'

'Anything else?'

She shook her head. 'What am I missing?'

'Look carefully at him the next time you see him. Maybe it will click.'

Christine arrived back. Set two small cups of espresso in front of us. 'Come sit down with us,' I said. 'What brought you here?'

'Worked as a secretary in the NHS — I wanted the opportunity to make a difference. Make a contribution to society. Had to leave — the pay was so poor. I saw an ad for this job. Got an interview and clicked with Mr Cooper. We seemed to think the same way. Been here two years now.'

'What about your home life?' I said. 'Partner? Children?'

'Been married for six years to a lovely man. Works as a chef at a country pub. Poor pay for long hours. We aren't really financially stable enough to think of children yet. Maybe in a year or so, or if I could make some money with a second job. It's always on our minds. A child would complete us. In the meantime, we're happy.'

'Never lose your dreams,' I said. 'Things have a habit of playing out if you give them time.'

'I never would have thought of me doing this job with a wonderful group of people a year ago,' Anji said. 'Enough to make you believe in fate.'

'I'll think of that,' Christine said. She looked at her watch. 'Gosh, how the time goes. I must get you to meet Ms Blair.'

We finished our small cups of coffee and followed her out of the room and along the corridor. Blair's office was at the far end opposite Cooper's. It was a large room with two black-topped tables, one as a desk and the other for larger gatherings. Ms Blair stood up as we entered. She was wearing the company blue colours with a pair of trousers flared at the bottoms. The difference for Blair was that she was wearing red high-heeled shoes. A small step for individuality; a giant leap against the conformity of the uniform.

We shook hands and made our introductions. She told us her first name was Susan, but we could call her Sue. She sat back down in her chair and steepled her fingers. Her muddy-brown hair was cut short in a pixie style. On her desk was a photo of her and a slim girl with blonde hair beyond her shoulders. It was taken somewhere exotic, with a long sandy beach with palm trees. A couple of what looked like rum punches, which signalled the Caribbean. Good for her. Work hard and play hard.

'First, before we start in earnest, I must make an apology,' I said. 'I'm going to bore you with a lot of questions, many of which may seem off the mark, but that's the nature of our game. Second, I'm going to take more time than you thought was possible.'

'I understand,' she said. 'I'm used to the annual audit. Picky, picky. Fire away.'

'It would help to know some background about you,' I said. 'What landed you here?'

'The twists and turns of fate,' she said. 'I studied accountancy at a polytechnic in the South Bank. Passed first class — *summa cum laude*. Served my time in a private practice. Stayed there for a long while until I realised I was never going to make partner — lacked the class or sex to make it through the glass ceiling. A job came up here and I took it — it was time to change the direction of my life. Been here five years now. Pretty good crew of people. Much more authority — I only report to Alan. What's next, Shannon? Do you want my eight discs to take on a desert island?'

'I did warn you about the questions,' I said. 'Who do you have under you?'

'Two ladies — account clerks — and a credit controller. They're solid. Worked with me after I had a clear out of the last lot that wasn't performing.'

'How much do you trust them? Any chance there has been hands in the till?'

'If there was, then the auditors should have picked it up. They say we're squeaky clean.'

'We will need access to all your accounts,' I said, 'log in codes and any other necessary passwords. We need remote access as well, so we can work off site. One more thing. Tell us everything about the planned extension.'

She got up from the desk and walked to a rolled-up tube by the side of a filing cabinet: too long to fit inside. She brought it back to the desk and unrolled it. Weighed it down with a coffee mug and the photo. 'These are the architect's plans. Nothing material will change, as we have planning permission. The architect will run the show, but will delegate the day-to-day running to a project manager. A structural engineer will make sure everything is safe, and the quantity surveyor will oversee buying all the materials at the lowest price.'

She placed her finger on the T-junction we had walked to earlier. 'The new extension will run from here. It will become a crossroads. On the right of the new building will be rooms for patients — thirty-four of them. On the left, at the top, will be an additional operating theatre and an enlarged pharmacy. There will be extra space for scanners — MRI and CAT. The rest will be offices for the additional load that will be created by the upsizing and more, and bigger, consulting rooms. The nurses will need their own rooms, too. It's a big project.'

'Impressive,' I said. 'How much will all this cost?'

'The estimate is twenty million—'

I whistled.

'—but these things always go over estimate and over time,' she said. 'That's why we need some outside investment. It's too rich for us alone. We reckon it will pay for itself in five years. After that, profits will soar. The government has committed nearly four billion pounds to hospital building and refurbishment. We want our share. This is cheaper and quicker than building a new hospital or upgrading existing ones.'

'Wow!' I said. 'Twenty million is still a lot of money. Who will be in charge at this end?'

'I'll deal with the money side, and Alan Cooper overseeing everything else. I think he'd need an extra person to handle it.'

I sat back in my chair, stunned by the amount of money involved.

'May I? said Anji.

'Go ahead,' I said.

'I love the picture,' she said. 'I've been trying to identify the cocktail. Rum punch or Mai Tai?'

'Mai Tai,' Blair said. 'You're good on your cocktails.'

'Sign of a misspent youth,' Anji said. 'The scenery looks like to die for. Saint Lucia is my guess. Not that I've ever been. Fat chance.'

'Barbados,' said Blair. 'Platinum coast. St James. Holiday of a lifetime. Maybe go back when I retire, which will be soon, I hope.'

'You don't look old enough for that,' Anji said. 'What are you? Forty-five?'

'A flattering guess. Clever girl. Fifty-two. I want to retire at fifty-five, so I'd better get some work done.'

'Many thanks,' I said. 'Do excuse us if we need to come back. We'll try to minimise any disruption. The sooner you can get us the codes, the better.'

We shook hands again and I studied her right hand. No rings there, but as I observed in the meeting, a wedding band on the left hand. No other jewellery I could see. We went back to our office and reviewed the meeting.

'Tell me what we have learned?' I said to Anji. 'Smart questioning, by the way.'

'Thank you. Shall we get the lesbian angle out of our way? It shouldn't make any difference to us and the job. I detect some resentment from her for not being able to get what she wanted,' she said. 'The thing about the glass ceiling.'

'And?'

'Can't be strapped for money if she can afford a holiday in Barbados, especially the Platinum coast. What else? Must be a ruthless streak — getting rid of the staff when she took over.'

'Of course, it may well be her partner who has the money,' I said.

'But that wouldn't help us much,' said Anji. 'The young girl in the photo doesn't seem the age to have money. Wedding band says she's serious about the relationship. Lucky lady — the girl looks dishy. Big age gap between the two of them. Might make a difference in the future.'

'What about now?' I said. 'What's her current state of mind?'

'She doesn't seem concerned about us digging through the accounts. Might that be that she is not up to anything illegal.'

'Could be a good poker player,' I said. 'Good at bluffing. I think that we will know more after we speak to her staff. They may be getting away with some scam that she hasn't picked up. This retirement thing in three years worries me. You need an awful lot of money to retire, especially since life expectancy is going up.'

Christine entered the room and smiled at us. 'The access codes and passwords you wanted,' she said, passing a slip of paper to me. 'I don't know what your plans are for lunch. We obviously have a kitchen for patients' meals, but that's not for staff use — one of those petty cost-saving measures that all managements like to impose. There's nothing close by but we do have a sandwich delivery. I could order you some.' She handed a menu to me. It was extensive. Time to try something different.

'I'll have a corned beef with horseradish and a pickled gherkin,' I said, 'on white.'

I handed the menu to Anji.

'Tuna mayo,' she said. 'On brown.'

I dug into my wallet and gave a ten-pound note to Christine.

'See you in half an hour,' she said. 'Do you want me to set up any more interviews?'

'We'll dig around for the rest of this morning,' I said, 'and then some meetings with people later today would be good — account clerks, credit controller. We'd also need to interview the consultants. Do it in the most efficient order. As many as feasible. Allow an hour each. Those we can't meet this afternoon, we'll start again in the morning.'

We logged on to their system and looked at the two most important parts — profit and loss account and balance sheet. Respectively, were they making any profit, and what assets did they have? What was in the bank? That wonderful thing everyone wants. Cash. We would look first at the last audited accounts and then at the current year. I called it up on my screen and told Anji how to get there.

At first glance, it seemed they were in good shape, but there was a lot of digging to be done. 'OK, Anji,' I said, playing mentor — it's the only way to learn. 'Tell me about the profit and loss account?'

'In the last full year — the one signed off by the auditors — they made a profit of three million pounds. I would call that good.'

'And what was the turnover?' I said.

'Revenue was thirty million, so a profit was ten per cent. Sounds fine by me.'

'What liquid assets do they have? I said. 'Tell me about the cash.'

'I can't see any,' Anji said.

'Then where is their three million of profit going?' I said.

'I got it,' she said triumphantly. 'Dividends. They're paying out the profits by dividends. There is no cash. The only asset worth mentioning is the building. Everything else goes into the pockets of the shareholders.'

'Check Companies House for shareholders,' I said. 'Strange that he and Blair didn't mention anything about shareholders or dividends. It's almost as though they're ashamed of what they're doing. Or they have something to hide. Call Norman and get him to do some digging. Let's park it for now and stretch our legs by having a walk around the grounds before lunch. Interesting, eh? Good morning's work. This afternoon, I'd like to see how much of the sales are NHS and how much are for the private clients. Are they dependent on the NHS or not? With the NHS in its current state, waiting lists getting longer, there will be a constant demand for the private sector.'

We logged off the system — couldn't have anyone coming into the office and have full control of it — and made our way downstairs. When we arrived at reception, there was an argument going on. A woman holding a bundle of cash was losing patience.

'I tell you I don't know his name, but he said if I don't pay with cash by Friday, then I would lose the discount.'

'We've encountered this scenario before,' I said to Anji. 'Time for you to fly solo. Off you go.'

Anji took a pad out of her bag and approached the woman. She smiled at her and took her aside. They talked for a couple of minutes and the woman, appeased, left the building, but not before handing over the cash to Anji.

'Let's have that walk now,' I said, 'and you can reveal all.'

We left the building and ambled over the grounds until we arrived at the scene of where the new building would be. Stood there taking it all in.

'It's like we've seen before,' Anji said. 'Common weakness. It's the credit control scam. The woman had a boob job done — made an initial payment with the rest to be paid monthly. She had a visit from a man who said if she paid off the balance in cash in one lump — if you pardon the unintended pun — she could have a thirty-three per cent discount. She got a short-term loan and decided to come here to pay it, rather than wait for a visit from the man — she had plans for Friday, so wouldn't be in.'

'How much was involved?' I said.

'The original operation was ten grand. She made a down payment of a grand, and the rest was supposed to be spread over the next five months.'

'Nine grand owing,' I said, 'and with a discount of a third, that would amount to a saving of three grand. You

21

could see why the woman was anxious to pay. She saw you as a person of authority and thought that you would sort everything out. Problem solved.'

'So we look at write-offs of bad debts next and then see the credit controller?' she said.

'Time for us to earn some money with a ten per cent share of any frauds found,' I said. 'The big question is whether Blair was in on the scam, or negligent in not spotting it.' I cast my eye over the T-junction of the building and where the new block was going. 'An extension here wouldn't harm the aesthetics. I can see why the planning people gave permission. The business rates would go up, so that's another incentive to pass it. Added local employment, too. All over bar the shouting.'

'I'm interested in finding out more about the cosmetic surgery side of the business,' Anji said. 'You hear so much about women going off to foreign climes to save money and have their operation there. Spend two weeks of recovery in the sun sipping Pina Coladas. Then there are the stories of everything going wrong and finishing off back on the NHS. Which way is the trend going?'

'I think we need to dig deep in the sales side of the accounts,' I said. 'See if there are any patterns. Domestic or foreign. Type of procedure or treatment. That kind of thing.'

I became silent as I gazed at the manicured lawn. This would be a good place to be for the birth of our twins. Peaceful, calm.

'I know it's not my role,' Anji said, 'and I'm very much a junior, but is there anything I can do to ease your peace of mind?'

'I was just thinking,' I said. 'I'm due to go with Cherry for the final scan tomorrow.'

'And you're worried about the results?'

'Uh huh.'

'You've got plenty of support from us. If the worse comes to the worst, I'm sure that Norman can deliver the babies and somehow make a profit.'

'Perish the thought,' I said, cracking a smile. 'I think that's a good place to end on.'

# CHAPTER THREE

Christine brought in our sandwiches and we asked her to arrange a meeting with the credit controller at three o'clock.

'Why three o'clock?' asked Anji. 'Why not now?'

'I want him to sweat a bit,' I said. 'Plus the fact that we need to be sure of our figures. Back to the accounts till then.'

Sure enough, the level of bad debts written off as non-collectable was higher than it should have been for a thriving business. Someone — Blair, Cooper, the auditors — should have picked it up. Or was it a blind eye being turned?

The credit controller's name was Andrew Jenkins. He stood up as we entered his small office. There was a picture of him on his desk, smiling with a yellow Lotus Elan convertible, second-hand, by the registration plate. *Vanity is thy sting?* This was a man who cared a lot about how others saw him.

He was tall, fit and toned. He had a full head of brown hair that fell over his forehead and he seemed to have to flick it from his left eye whenever he turned his head. I would have found it exasperating and resorted to a haircut, but it gave him the chance of being seen with a roguish element to his handsome face. I imagined that it might appeal to a woman looking forward to mothering his child-like aura. He had green eyes and long eyelashes. His teeth were as white as it was possible to get and flashed each time he smiled. The smile was like that of a crocodile before it eats you.

We made our introductions during which he ogled Anji a little longer than necessary.

'So you're the fabled Shannon,' he said. 'What an honour.'

'You probably know a lot about me,' I said, 'much of it hyped up, so maybe we can start with some background about you. Tell us your story?'

'Not much to say,' he said. 'Joined the army after school. Flat feet, so not suitable for action. I spent ten years in the clerical section of the marines. After my last tour of duty, my time deserved to come to an end. The marines guided me to a background course in finance, and I got an accounts clerk job here. I was promoted to credit controller a year ago. I'm unmarried, so I can please myself on what I can spend my salary — you've seen the picture. I like fast cars and fast women. Not a bad life, eh?'

'Depends where you get your money,' I said. 'Tell us, how long have you been pulling the scam?'

The smile disappeared. A bead of sweat formed on his forehead.

'Three grand today,' I said. 'Nice little earner. Like I said, how many times have you pulled the scam? What's the grand total of your fraud?'

'I don't know what you're talking about,' he said.

'Show him the cash, Anji.'

Anji placed the cash on the table and riffled through the notes for effect.

'Don't get tedious on me,' I said. 'I'm losing patience. How much?'

'It was more like a loan,' he said. 'The Lotus came up for sale. Great condition. Lovely price. It was too good an opportunity to miss. I needed some cash to afford it. I was going to pay it back. I swear.'

'With all you've read about me,' I said, 'do you think I would fall for such a cock-and-bull story? If you pardon the cliché, the game's up. How much?'

'It was about thirty grand, that's all. Hardly noticeable. A tick on an elephant's hide, for this business.'

'You realise we have to report this,' I said.

'Don't do that,' he whined. 'It will ruin my career. What if I said you could keep that cash? No one need know. I'd sell the Lotus, too. Chip in with what I make for that?'

'You've seen the news about me — can't be ignored. You've read all the articles about me in the papers, all the viral videos. What's the one word that they say of me?'

He thought for a moment. 'Honour,' he said. 'That you hold honour more than anything else.'

'And what would turning a blind eye be?' I said.

'Without honour,' he said. 'You're going to report me.'

'Better start to find a cardboard box and pack up your things,' I said. 'You can try to prepare your speech, but I don't think you will sway Blair or Cooper. Nice teeth, by the way.'

We got up and left him sitting there in silence, pondering his fate.

* * *

Time to break the bad news to Cooper. With Anji behind me, I knocked on his door and following Christine's example and Cooper's door-always-open principle, opened it and walked straight in. The office was empty. Maybe a confidential chat? I knocked on that door — I felt that what we had to say was important. No answer. I went to the door to the wet room. Again, I knocked on the door, waited and opened it.

Hellfire! Cooper was lying on the floor, a syringe in his right hand and five empty ones on the floor beside him. Blood was coming from his head. His lips and fingers were tinged blue. I knew what that meant. It wasn't good. He was barely breathing. I didn't give him much time on this earth.

'Your screaming is probably better than mine,' I said to Anji. 'Get help.'

She ran through to the office door, flung it open and screamed 'Help!' She continued shouting as loud as she could until one of the nurses heard her. I could hear some-one running along the corridor. 'Here!' she shouted this time. 'Quick! Inside!'

I took the nurse through to the wet room.

'Oh, God!' she said. She picked up one of the syringes on the floor and looked at it. 'I'll do what I can,' she said. 'Run to the pharmacy and get naloxone. As much as there is. It's his only chance.'

Anji ran out of the office. The nurse put her head on Cooper's chest. I noticed that there was little rise and fall, almost no breathing. I knew in my heart he wasn't going to make it. Another job for Palmer: boy, was he going to like this. I prepared myself for some vitriol.

I took out my mobile phone and pressed on his name in 'favourites' and that said a lot. He answered straightaway — must be a slow day. I told him the circumstances and that he would need SOCO and the police doctor. I heard him sigh and he broke the connection.

Anji reappeared. 'There's no naloxone,' she said. 'I can't find any. There's just an empty place on the shelf where the label is.'

'I'll get a doctor,' the nurse said. 'Try to keep him awake.'

She stood up and ran from the room.

I started shouting at Cooper. No response. I slapped him across the face. Two times, three times, four. There was no reaction. Then he opened his eyes and stared at me as if to say, *why me?* It was the last thing he did. Cooper had gone to meet his maker. The gold cross on his lapel seem to shine mockingly at me. *No more philosophy,* it seemed to say.

A doctor came and examined Cooper. He shook his head. 'Nothing I can do,' he said.

'Leave him here,' I said. 'Don't touch anything in the room. The police will be here soon. They will want to pre-serve the scene.'

I stood up and went out of the wet room door. Anji followed me to the main office. We looked through the big windows, stared out at the car park and waited. Time didn't matter any more.

* * *

'You've done it again, Shannon,' Palmer said when he entered Cooper's office. 'Another dead body to notch up on your bedpost.'

'He doesn't do it on purpose,' Anji said, defending me. 'He sort of acts as a catalyst. Makes things happen.'

'Some people don't like what we do,' I said. 'They're afraid of what we might find out. There's something happening here and I'm going to find out what it is. It's part of our contract and I have to see it through to the end. To break a contract would be to act without honour. I can't do that.'

Palmer sighed. 'I'm never going to work you out, Shannon, but what I do understand is that you're a man of principle. I like that. The world would be a better place if it had more principles. Now,' he said, 'SOCO will be here in a little while. We might as well make best use of the time. What have we got? Bears all the signs of suicide to me. Injects himself with a fatal dose, goes unconscious, falls over and hits his head on the basin, thus, the head wound.'

'That's what we are meant to believe,' I said. 'First off, what killed him? Look at the blue tinges to his lips and fingers.'

'Give in,' Palmer said.

'Overdose of morphine.'

'How do you know that?' Palmer asked.

'Remember the case at the solicitors? Ackroyd being poisoned? I did some research on poisons after that. The blue tinges are a classic sign of morphine overdose.'

'Whatever. But he's lying here with a syringe in his hand,' Palmer protested. 'Seems obvious.'

'Come with me,' I said. I moved to the guitar. Picked it up and strummed the first lines of "Woodstock". Easy song. Just two chords. 'Well,' I said. 'What do you think of that?'

'That you should get out more,' Palmer said. 'OK. Sounds fine.'

'You know what happened to me in prison. Two fingers on my left hand lost to an act of revenge. So how do I manage to play the guitar?'

'Ah,' said Palmer. 'I get it.'

'He's restrung the guitar so he can play left-handed. And what hand is the syringe in?'

'Right,' said Palmer. 'The wrong hand.'

'Precisely,' I said. 'It's all been staged. Plus the fact that all the naloxone — the antidote — is missing.'

'Any clues on a murderer? Anyone on your list?'

'We've only just started,' I said.

'We do have someone running a scam,' said Anji, 'but it doesn't seem big enough to murder someone. Am I right?'

'Yes,' I said. 'To kill someone, there must be something big going on. The only question is what?'

'Take care,' he said. 'You're a lucky man. Let's hope the luck doesn't run out. What's your secret? Do you believe in unicorns?'

'Only when I dream.'

'I thought so,'

'But I dream a lot.'

'I'd expect nothing less.'

# CHAPTER FOUR

Palmer asked if I would like to come along to see Cooper's wife, and my curiosity won against the pressure I would face from Cherry to drop the investigation. Palmer, a female sergeant in uniform, and I parked in front of Cooper's house and sat there surveying it. Putting off breaking the bad news as long as we could.

The house was detached and looked like it had some character. It was in Islington and so worth a pretty penny. A couple of million pounds was my uneducated guess. It was well maintained; no peeling paint or signs of rotten wood. It had been well looked after. Finally, we got out of Palmer's car and rang the bell. A dog barked. Locks undone. Chain slid out. The door opened.

It was the policewoman who caught her eye among the three of us. Mrs Cooper's face went pale. Her shoulders sagged. She stared at some point in the middle distance, unwilling to believe what was happening. What was about to happen. I felt for her.

Palmer made the introductions, Mrs Cooper recognising me from the news reports, and asked her if we could come in. She led us into a wide hall with a split staircase going up and then branches to the left and right, and through a door into the living room. It was large and full of light due to windows on two sides and French doors into the garden. There were three two-seater sofas and one bigger at three seats. They were in a classic print featuring flowers and exotic birds of some description which I couldn't identify. Or maybe they had just been made up — lots of life is made up nowadays. One wall was papered in a faux Beardsley print and the other three in a light terracotta. Tasteful. A nice room to relax with a gin and tonic when home from work.

Mrs Cooper — Audrey, she said to call her — was a tall, slim woman of around fifty. Her hair was auburn and streaked with highlights and lowlights, whatever those latter were. She was wearing a pair of denim jeans with a white shirt tied at the waist and her hair bunched back in a pony tail. I wondered whether we had interrupted her in the act of cleaning.

'Do sit down,' said Palmer.

'Something bad has happened, hasn't it?' she said.

'I'm afraid your husband died this afternoon,' Palmer said. 'You have our deepest sympathies.'

'I'll make some tea,' said the sergeant, preparing for the time when all she must do was comfort.

'How did he die?' Audrey said. 'Heart attack? Stroke?'

'It's early days in our investigation,' Palmer said, 'but we think he was poisoned. Did Alan have any enemies?'

'No,' she said. 'He was a deeply Christian man. Cared deeply about people. Enemies? Unthinkable. He was a pillar of the community. Did so much for the church. Everybody loved him. Everybody respected him.'

'What were his hobbies?' Palmer said. 'We need to understand him and see what the motive was.'

'It was mostly things to do with the church — bell ringing, keeping the books. He did play bridge once every week.'

'Regular partner?' I said.

'Yes,' she said, 'woman called Noreen.'

'Give her contact details to the sergeant and that of the club chairman,' Palmer said. 'We'll need to speak to them.'

'Did he go out much?' I said. 'Socialise? Down the pub for chicken and chips and a pint with the lads?'

'He was vegan,' she said. 'We used to go out for a meal once a month, but Alan got fed up with the lack of choice — cauliflower ten ways, he used to say.'

'Was he worried about anything at work?' Palmer asked.

'Not that he said. We rarely talked about his work — he liked to compartmentalise work and home life. Now I think about it, though, he did seem a little distracted lately. I think the preparations for the new extension may have been weighing on his mind. It was a big project and very important to him. He saw it in a social way — opening up a new stream of NHS patients to relieve the pressure it faced — as well as from a pure business sense.'

'Any money worries?' I said. 'Credit cards maxed or mortgage problems?'

'We paid off the mortgage years ago,' she said. 'Alan didn't like debt — neither a lender or borrower be, he used to say. We have a simple life. To be frank, there's not anything that we want for. We pay into a pension scheme each month, so the future is secured. His salary covers all we need. We have good holidays three times a year.'

Tears started forming in her eyes. The weight of the truth was starting to bear down on her. 'Excuse me,' she said, getting out of her seat and walking out of the door.

'It's sinking in,' Palmer said. 'Thankfully, I don't have much exposure to this kind of scene. Jane — the Community Policing officer — will know more about that. We don't get many instances like this: most deaths are for stabbings and shootings.'

'It's a wild world out there,' I said.

'And you've tried to make a difference. Your youth-club experience with Buzz is trying to get the kids off the streets, and keep them from feeling there was no gang uniform without a knife. You've made a difference.'

Audrey came back in the room. Her eyes were red; her nose, too. She was carrying a box of man-size tissues and sat back on the sofa. It was an awkward moment.

Tea arrived. The policewoman handed Audrey a cup. 'I managed to find some brandy in the kitchen,' Jane said, 'so I added a little of that plus three spoons of sugar. Drink every drop.'

'We want to find the killer quickly,' Palmer said. 'Every hour that passes means catching the murderer gets less likely, more time for the killer to cover his or her tracks. With your permission, we'd like to make a search of any computers or paperwork he had.'

'Of course,' she said. 'His study is in the bedroom at the front.'

'Do you have any children here?' I said.

'Flown the nest,' she said. 'I'll have to tell them soon before the news hits the papers, won't I?'

'Jane will make the initial calls, if you like,' Palmer said.

'Is there anyone who could come and help you get over the next few days?' I said. 'Lend a hand with the practicalities? Provide some emotional support?'

'Sally next door is a good friend. She won't mind spending some time with me. Would Alan have died without pain?' she said, with no segue.

'Yes,' Palmer said. 'He wouldn't have known anything about it. It was an overdose of morphine. He would have been totally calm before his death. His breathing would just have dropped until he could draw no more. We'll pop upstairs and have a look round. Jane, here, will keep bringing you cups of tea and provide you with a listening ear.'

'Why is Shannon here?' she said. 'Isn't he involved in frauds? Do you think there was something illegal that Alan was involved in? Blackmail?'

'I wouldn't worry about that,' Palmer said, avoiding any commitment. 'Come, Shannon. Let's go upstairs.'

Palmer and I went upstairs and found Cooper's study in the bedroom looking out on the street. There was a pinboard on the wall facing Cooper. I looked through the items on it, but there was nothing of interest — dental appointments, timetable of church events — all very innocent. Palmer slid a drawer out of one of two filing cabinets and started to search through for what we did not know.

On the desktop, there was a plastic three-drawer holder marked 'in', 'out' and 'pending'. I took the papers out of the 'in' drawer, which was topmost. There were several statements for accounts at three different banks. There was a lot in ISAs deposited to the maximum over a good few years. The rest of their money was spread across fixed-term investments over one to three years and instant access savings accounts. They had plenty in savings. At first glance, there didn't seem to be any large deposits indicating blackmail in some form. He was an ordinary guy. There seemed to be no reason for him to die. He was virtually a recluse outside the church and one evening a week at the bridge club. Whatever it was, it would be work-related.

The fate of the credit controller would now be in Blair's hands. I'd need to fill her in on the scam. How would she react? Did she have the milk of human kindness to forgive and forget? What would be the outcome in terms of dividends, assuming Cooper had been a shareholder? Bigger share for everybody else? *Mucho pesetas* for the remaining shareholders?

The 'out' tray was basically for things he hadn't got round to filing. Telephone bills, energy statements, that kind of thing. 'Pending' was for items he had yet to get around to do, which wasn't much. He seemed on top of all his finances. There was a subscription renewal request for *Private Eye* which said 'No renewal. Blasphemy.' Some religious joke that didn't go down well with him, no doubt.

'How are you doing?' I said to Palmer.

'Nothing,' he said. 'You?'

'He's squeaky clean. Lots of money spread across various banks. Credit cards settled in full each month. He had no money problems. Blind alley. One moment.' I paused while I checked. 'There's a printout of a spreadsheet in the pending file. A list of all the employees and consultants — some have got black dots against them; some have question marks. Might be relevant if we can crack what they mean. I'll take it for study later. Nothing worth investigating among all the other papers.'

'Let's take the laptop and hope that there is something useful in that,' Palmer said. 'We'll use the same procedure — we go to your place and you download everything and then I'll hand it over to our boffins. You know what you're looking for; they don't. Should give you an edge.'

'And, boy, don't we need one?'

* * *

The atmosphere was hostile when Palmer and I got home. Something was brewing, and I knew what it was. There was silence while I got Valentine to copy what was on the hard drive of Cooper's laptop. I gave Palmer the computer, and he hurried off to another spoiled dinner.

'I want to talk to you,' Cherry said as soon as we were alone, which she manipulated well. She had me cornered in my office while everyone was in the river room.

'Anji has told me what happened today. Another death on a job. You promised you would quit if there was any danger to any of us. What do you say, man of honour?'

'I only need till the end of the week,' I said. 'It's an easy-peasy job. The auditor signed off the accounts two months ago.'

'And they missed the credit controller scam? What comfort can I take from that? What else might they have missed? Does danger increase in any more digging? Answer me that.'

'It's a hospital, and from what I've seen, a well-run one, too. I don't expect to find anything else. The credit control scam is a petty one that has no bearing on the business as a whole.'

'So why was Cooper murdered?' Cherry said. 'Unless it had something to do with his home life, there's a killer lurking somewhere. Anji told me it was a massive dose of morphine. Anyone could have gained access to the pharmacy. The field's wide open. You may already have met the killer.'

'I have Palmer on my side,' I said. 'Surely that makes a difference? Harming me would be like an attack on the police, and you know how seriously they take that. I'd be well protected. And I can always get Arthur to shadow me, too. I can finish this job by the end of the week. Just give me till then. Four days is all I ask.'

'What about the rest of us?' she said. 'You know what happened the last time there was a murder. I finished up with an arrow in my back and in ICU.'

'Anji can work from here. Nobody else here needs to visit the hospital bar me. You can all stay here safe. Arthur could always look out for all of you instead of me.'

'Is it worth the risk so as purely not to break the contract, so as to satisfy your honour code?'

'Four days, Cherry. That's all I ask.'

'Oh, Shannon,' she said. 'Why do you do this to me? Four days. Granted. No more. And if anything goes wrong, I will hold you responsible. I'll spend the next four days dreaming up the worst punishment I can do to you. You might as well take whoever you need, if it gets the job finished more quickly.'

'Why do I do it to you?' I said. 'Because you always support me. Because I love you, that's why.'

'Don't pull that old one,' she said. 'It won't wash today.'

CHAPTER FIVE

I was at the police station at eight o'clock. It was going to be
a busy schedule and I wanted to be ahead of what the day
might bring. Anji was going to Fairstead with Arthur holding
her hand. She would get everything from the HM depart-
ment about all the staff. We needed to see if we could crack
Cooper's code of black dots and question marks. Why HM, I
wondered? Human managing? Managing humans? Sounded
like some dystopia in science fiction. Whatever. Bring home
everything, laptops included, that we might need to work
remotely back at the office.

The desk sergeant looked at me with a puzzled expression. 'Wasn't expecting to see you,' he said.

'What do you mean?' I said. 'I have to come every day
— that's the deal.'

'DCI Palmer said that while you are working with him
on the Cooper case that would count as a daily report. You're
a caged bird set free.'

I went back home and had a coffee while Cherry got
ready for the ten o'clock appointment at our local NHS hospital. There seemed to be no need to go private. Everything
was pretty much normal.

She spent a lot of time applying what little make-up she used and I guessed that was to compensate for her current self-image of whale/hippopotamus. She wore a loose-fitting long black dress and kitten heels and, to me, looked like a million dollars.

We were outside visiting hours and ahead of the peak outpatient slots and managed to find a parking bay without too much trouble. Hallelujah! We logged in at the main reception desk and were shunted to the first of the waiting areas. There were lots of people in white coats or nurses' uniforms milling around without, it seemed, much of a purpose. When Cherry's name appeared on the screen, we moved to the next waiting area. I was beginning to feel there must be a better way. The seats were low-budget utilitarian and I hoped we wouldn't have to stay too long. Cherry wriggled around. Every now and again she jumped when one of the twins kicked her.

Finally, we were fed through to a small room with all the equipment needed for what should be the last scan before delivery. Two people were there: a young female nurse and an imposing man with a mane of ginger hair and full beard. The long hair partly — but only partly — concealed a cauliflower ear, presumably from a rugby injury. He introduced himself with a Scottish trill as consultant gynaecologist Stuart Ferguson. He was wearing grey slacks, a blazer with gold buttons and black brogues — handmade, probably, going by the size of his feet. He had large fingers, which would seem to be a disadvantage to someone doing intricate operations. I brushed the thought aside.

Cherry pulled up her dress to reveal the bump and laid down on a couch. There was a lot of lubricant applied and a monitor stood ready to reveal all. I watched the monitor, not knowing what I should be looking for. Then a thrill when I could make out the two figures that would be our twins. The nurse took a picture for us to keep.

Ferguson frowned. My heart started beating faster.

'I don't know whether you wanted a natural delivery, but I would like to do a Caesarean. You're older than normal, for one thing — post thirty-five, there is a greater risk of complications, plus the fact that it is twins. Also, only one of the babies is in the right position. Nothing to worry much about, but I'd like to err on the safe side.'

I could sense that Cherry was disappointed and, like me, no need to worry much sounded like there was a need to worry at least some.

'I'd like to do the C-section myself,' Ferguson said. 'Not that my registrar isn't capable of doing it — it's quite a common procedure — but, as I said, I'd like to err on the safe side. Not wishing to be seen as drumming up work for myself, I would recommend coming in to Fairstead where I have my private practice. It would be so much more comfortable for your post-op care. I understand, Mr Shannon, that you are working there at the moment. Reassure Mrs Shannon of the impressive nature of everything there.'

Cherry looked at me with fear in her eyes. In the light of Cooper's death, it was probably the last place she wanted to be. But the babies had to be put above everything else.

'It's peaceful and serene,' I said. 'You'd be comfortable there. All the facilities are modern and there has been no expense spared with all the necessary technology. Plus, we've got a few weeks for the current situation to be resolved. If it's good for the twins, that's the only thing that counts.'

'I suppose so,' Cherry said, clearly not happy in her heart.

'Believe me,' Ferguson said, 'it's a safe place to go to. You couldn't be in better hands anywhere else. Take it easy, Mrs Shannon, and I'll see you in a few weeks. As for you, Mr Shannon, mollycoddle her. Don't let her lift a finger. Soon you'll be a proud father.'

'Thank you,' I said. 'I'm hoping to catch you at Fairstead to talk over the business and the new extension.'

'My secretary will be in touch about any slots in my diary.' Ferguson said. 'Take care.'

Cherry took a handful of tissues from the nurse and wiped away the remaining lubricant. She stood up, pulled her dress down and we left the room in silence.

There was a coffee shop in the main reception area and I steered Cherry to it. There were things that needed to be talked about, and shouldn't wait till we were back in the car and my concentration elsewhere. While in the queue I googled *Stuart Ferguson gyn* and found he had a website. He was described as 'eminent' and had several papers published in learned journals on endometriosis. I was reassured of his capabilities. I got two coffees — espresso for me and a black with oat milk for Cherry. We found a table and sat ourselves down. I passed my phone to Cherry.

'They say he's one of the best gynaecologists around,' I said. 'Look at his credentials. Couldn't want for a better CV.'

When she finished reading his profile, she looked at me with a tear in her eye. 'Complications,' she said. 'I don't want complications. I want to be a normal pregnant woman going through a normal journey to a normal motherhood. Normal everything. Why can't that be the case?'

'Ferguson is just playing safe,' I said. 'Better safe than sorry. I'd rather that than being unprepared for something that crops up at the last minute. I'm sure everything will be fine. He's just trying to cover all the angles.'

'But Fairstead,' she said. 'You don't know what's lurking under the surface.'

'I'm only concerned about the finance side. There's nothing to suggest there's anything wrong with the medical side. On the contrary, it seems to be excellent. I can arrange for you to come with me and have a tour.'

'I dare say they do a good facelift, but I'm concerned with birthing,' she said.

'With Ferguson in charge, I think nothing can go wrong. You'd be in capable hands.'

'I'm sure you're right,' she said. 'Perhaps I'm just a natural worrier. Well, this coffee is disgusting. Why did you let me have oat milk? Let's go and try to have a normal day while we can.'

We walked — waddled — back to the Beamer and set off back home. Anji was back from Fairstead and was sitting at my conference desk surrounded by buff manila folders, acquired, no doubt, from HR. 'How's it going?' I asked.

'Do you know how many work there?' she said.

I shook my head.

'Like infinity,' she said, 'it's one more than you thought.'

'Try starting with consultants and work down from there,' I said. 'See if there's any connection with Cooper's code. Start a spreadsheet so we can do multiple analyses and hope something stands out. Get Valentine to help you. Two brains are probably better than one and it's likely to be tedious, so it's easy to lose concentration. If anything jumps out, call me immediately.'

* * *

I set off to Fairstead and ran through what I might do during the day. Palmer was there in Cooper's office, waiting for me.

'You took your time, Shannon,' he said. 'Everything OK?'

'There are complications,' I said, 'but there's nothing we can do bar change our plans.'

We ducked under the yellow tape and looked around the office.

'What's the latest?' I said.

'SOCO has finished with their examination,' Palmer said, 'so we can go in without fear of compromising the murder scene.'

'What has SOCO taken of the contents of the office?' I asked.

'There's the laptop and papers from yesterday. Phone — there's some wonderful things they can do to unlock it and scour the contents. Diary, if he had a paper one running alongside a digital one. They'll have photographed the whole scene and examined contents of the desk and wastepaper bin. We can touch anything without spoiling any evidence.'

'So bottom line,' I said, 'is whatever has been left they'll have looked at already?'

'But you have a different mind to them,' Palmer said. 'Sneaky. You'll see the importance of what they might not even consider.'

The floor had numbered yellow plaques on it where evidence had been photographed and logged.

'Time of death?' I said.

'Christine brought in his sandwich — tofu and plant-based mayo — at twelve thirty. The sandwich was eaten' — he picked a brown paper bag from the bin — 'and analysis of stomach contents will confirm that, and see if there is anything else of interest. The doctor says that Cooper had probably died around half two, although there's a margin of error on that. To be on the safe side, we're looking at one o'clock onwards.'

Palmer took a seat in Cooper's chair and I sat opposite. He gazed at the desktop and leafed through a pile of manila folders. He straightened them up to his satisfaction and passed them over to me.

'Technical stuff,' he said. 'More your expertise than mine. Can you make any sense of it?'

'I'll photocopy everything and look through it later,' I said. 'You can hand the originals in.'

Christine came into the room. 'This may sound insensitive, but would you like me to order you a sandwich?'

She handed a menu to Palmer.

'Do they have napkins?' he asked.

'I'm sure they could handle that,' Christine said.

'Ham and pickle on brown, no spread,' he said.

'Salt beef and English mustard on white,' I said.

'Anything else I can do for you?' she said. 'Without Mr Cooper here, I'm at a bit of a loss for things to do.'

'You could arrange for these files to be photocopied, please. That would be marvellous,' I said.

I passed the files to her.

'Was there anything unusual in Mr Cooper's behaviour yesterday?' I asked. 'Anything out of the ordinary?'

'Cast your mind back,' said Palmer. 'What was he doing yesterday?'

'In the morning, he was reading these files. I brought him a coffee about eleven, and he seemed absorbed in something. Hardly said a word when I gave him the coffee.'

'And after that?' I said.

'He said he'd like anything vegan for his sandwich — didn't mind what. I got him tofu and plant-based mayo. Took it in to him about half past eleven. Hardly looked up from the papers, like he couldn't waste a moment.'

'What about the afternoon?' said Palmer. 'When was the last time you saw him?'

'I didn't see him in the afternoon. He never took tea. I was working on typing up a big report for him. Couldn't finish it before it was time to go home. No reason to go into his office, especially when he seemed to be concentrating so hard.'

'And you didn't see anyone go into his office at any stage of the afternoon?' I said.

'Like I said, I had my head down typing away.'

'We'd like a copy of the report, please,' I said.

'What was strange, though,' she said, 'was that I heard him playing the guitar. Spanish music.'

'What time was this?' Palmer asked.

'It started about two, and went on for about forty-five minutes. He didn't usually play guitar to himself. Only when he was serenading a distressed client in their room. He worried that it might discourage someone to come into the room.'

'Thank you,' said Palmer. 'And don't forget the napkins.'

She almost curtseyed in front of Palmer as she left the room.

'From what Christine said, it would look like time of death anywhere after two forty-five. Later than we thought,' I said.

'Scenario: the killer goes into the office, thumps Cooper with a blow to the head and knocks him out,' Palmer said. 'He drags him into the en suite and starts injecting Cooper with a lethal dose of morphine. Slips away when the deed is done.'

'I wonder if you need any experience in injecting someone.' I said. 'If you do, then we could limit any enquiries to doctors and nurses.'

'Something to check out,' he said. 'I'll leave that one to you.'

'Did SOCO find the murder weapon?' I said. 'Something heavy.'

Palmer cast his eyes around the room. 'SOCO didn't find anything, and looking around the room here, nothing stands out.'

'So the killer brings his own weapon,' I said. 'Which means he has to get rid of it. Is it worth doing a search of the grounds?'

'I have a feeling it would be fruitless,' Palmer said, 'but we have to do it anyway.'

'One thing,' I said. 'We keep talking of *him*. We know that poison is a woman's choice, but that is usually because a woman introduces the poison into food. We can't rule out a woman here.'

'Accepted,' Palmer said. 'Be objective at all times.'

'Pass me the bin,' I said. 'I'll go through that while you check the drawers.'

He handed me the plastic wastepaper bin, very gratefully! Nothing messy for him to go through.

There was the brown paper bag that had held the sandwich. It had crusts inside. Very picky. Palmer shuddered as I placed it on the desktop which he had made so neat and tidy. There were a couple of crumpled up things-to-do sheets on A4 paper which combined domestic duties — more food for the dog and so on — as well as items related to the business, but those were not significant. Nothing in bold or underlined. Blair's name was on one of them, and I wondered if he had any idea about what might have been going on in credit control. Good to be able to establish that later. There was a credit card slip for a lunch at some Italian restaurant, as if he had been sorting out his wallet. I took it and put it on a separate pile to be studied later. At first glance, the itemised bill was a mixture of vegan dishes and one for someone who liked fish. Only two drinks had been taken — small glasses of Pinot Grigio.

'Did SOCO find a wallet?' I asked Palmer.

'If one was here, then they would have taken it. I'll check when I get back to the office. You'd want to find out what was in it, I presume?' Palmer said.

'Why don't you make a call now? I said. 'Time may be of the essence.'

He gave a sigh as if I was dragging him away from a train of thought that might be crucial. I continued to rake through the bin, adding to the discarded contents on the desktop. A bead of perspiration broke out on Palmer's forehead.

Palmer put his phone down. 'SOCO found a Filofax,' he said. 'Cooper was a great organiser, it seems. Wrote everything down in the diary section. Once they've made some notes and photographed anything that could be crucial, they'll send it over to us. Back to the desk drawers.'

My analysis of the bin finished with nothing else material having been found. I got up from the desk and walked across to the door of the private room and looked inside. The table was bare apart from a Mont Blanc fountain pen in rose gold. Why the pen when nothing to write on? Security? Make sure nobody steals the valuable pen when he was out of the office?'

'Ah ha!' said Palmer. 'What have we here?'

He was looking at the topmost drawer on the left-hand side. I couldn't see what he was looking at. Before I got up to get a view, the sounds of Spanish guitar filled the room. Bingo!

'That's it!' said Christine, bursting into the room. 'That's what I heard. Lovely, isn't it?'

'Paco Pena,' I said, 'if I'm not mistaken. "Memories of the Alhambra". Guy next door to me in the hall of residence used to play it incessantly. I've not been keen on it since then. Excess of riches.'

Palmer took the cassette player from the drawer and placed it on the desk. 'Job for SOCO,' he said. 'We just might have some fingerprints here.'

'Cancel the sandwiches,' I said. 'We're going out to lunch.' I looked at the credit card slip. 'Nene Maria. Ever heard of it, Christine?'

'Sure,' she said. 'It was Mr Cooper's favourite near here. Used to take staff there when he wanted to discuss matters of so much importance that they had be talked about outside of this building. Away from anyone's ears.'

'When he went out to lunch,' I said, 'did you know who his guest was?'

'No,' she said. 'He was so very secretive that he would leave on his own and the other person — whoever it was — would follow him five minutes later, so you never knew who it was.'

'While we're gone, could you set up a meeting with Ms Blair for three o'clock? DCI Palmer and I have a few questions we need to ask her. Tell her it is police business and that no other time would be possible. Put the photocopies and the report you were typing on the desk and don't touch anything in here. This is still a crime scene.'

Christine nodded and exited the room. Palmer and I rose from our chairs and left for lunch with more questions than answers. But first, I took the photo of Cooper that was on the desk. Be prepared.

* * *

Nene Maria's was a ten-minute walk away and wasn't doing much business. It was one o'clock and I had assumed it would be full of diners. Never a good sign — indicator of poor cooking. We sat down without great expectations. Very Dickensian. Would Pip save the day?

The restaurant walls were terracotta, the tablecloths a deep red to add a contrast. There were empty straw-covered bottles of chianti hanging from the ceiling and fishing nets in three corners of the room. All in all, typical Italian. I bet they had a two-feet high pepper grinder.

The menu was extensive, which again was a bad sign. How could a chef handle such a long list without generous use of a freezer and, latterly, microwave? We ordered two glasses of Barolo while we were making our selection.

'Steak and chips for me, no starter, no salad,' Palmer said to the waitress. She was dark-haired with blonde highlights that seemed inappropriate for a girl coming from Italian genes, and I wondered whether this was a family business and she was sucked into it.

'Osso bucco for me,' I said. It had been a long time since I had tasted slowly cooked beef. It should really be veal, but there was little call for that due to qualms about the short lives of the young cow.

'Right,' Palmer said. 'What have we got?'

'Your boffins have got the phone,' I said, 'maybe they can extract something from that. Frequent calls over the last week, say, contacts, texts and so on that he made before he was killed, that sort of thing. What we do have now is the cassette player — that might yield fingerprints. If the killer wore gloves, then that might be a blind alley.'

'And what is there in abundance in a hospital?' Palmer said. 'Protective coverings. Including gloves. It would be like a needle in a haystack to find the pair the killer used.'

'If Christine heard the music at two,' I said, 'then it would have been the last thing the killer would have done before exiting the office. I would think then that the time of death can now be estimated just prior to two o'clock.

'Your forensic people will have the diary, too,' I continued. 'Maybe something in there. Be good to have a look at it when they're finished. There are people I need to talk with to satisfy the final report on the project. How do you want to play it? Me going solo or you tagging along?'

'You lead,' he said. 'I'll follow. Anything I should know?'

'There's a small fraud that has been going on. Fiddle on credit control. Thirty grand the miscreant has claimed. I think it's more than that, but there's no easy way to prove it. That was why I wanted to see Cooper that afternoon; Ms Blair should not be aware of it. Let's see how she reacts.'

The waitress came along to take our plates. Clean. The food had been good, after all. Don't be too quick to judge, Shannon.

'You're slow today. Is this normal?' I asked her.

'Our trade is biased towards the evening. Slow for lunch, but giving time for the chefs to prepare for dinner.'

'A friend of mine recommended you to us.' I dug out the photo of Cooper and family. 'Do you recognise him?'

'Mr Cooper,' she said. 'He is a regular, but never alone.'

'He would have come here last week,' I said. 'Can you remember who dined with him?'

'I had not seen the man before,' she said.

'Can you describe him?' Palmer said. He got out his warrant card. 'Police. Anything you tell us will be in strict confidence.'

'He was tall and handsome,' she said. 'Brown hair, receding at the temples. He was dressed in a blue suit. That's all.'

'Thank you,' I said. 'You've been very helpful.' She hadn't, unfortunately, but what's the point saying otherwise?

'Do you want to know about the other one?' she said.

'The other one?' said Palmer. 'What do you mean?'

'He came on Tuesday, too,' she said. 'Dowdy woman in red shoes. They talk low, as if it was a dark secret, even though there were only a few people in here'

This time, she was helpful. I left her a ten-pound tip.

As we walked back, we had a spring in our step. Avenues for questioning had opened up for us. We had an unknown man and Susan Blair to interview. Our arrangement for the three o'clock appointment with Blair had potential. I filled Palmer in on my interview with her and the credit card fraud that had been taking place. We agreed that I should start with the fraud and how much she knew about it, and then he would take over on the lunch date and the murder.

She sat calmly in her office when we entered. She stood steadily when we approached her desk. Her hands didn't tremble as she shook Palmer's hand. I didn't qualify for a handshake. Boo hoo. You can't make friends with everyone.

'I have some bad news for you,' I said. 'Andrew Jenkins has been cheating on you. It's not an unusual fraud — we come across it several times in a year — writing off debtors for a big discounted wodge of cash. I can't say how long it has been going or the total amount he has made on it. His story is that it has only been going on for a few months and the total is about thirty thousand. What is your reaction?'

She wrung her fingers together — not so cocky now, Blair, huh? 'I'm surprised,' she said. 'No, "shocked" could be a better word. Andrew gave all evidence of being a loyal and honest employee. Did he say why he did it?'

'The classic factors of needing the money and pulling the wool over the eyes of the system,' I said. 'Stick it to the man. Cheap thrill.'

'I'll have to consider this deeply,' she said, leaning back in her chair.

'For why?' I said. 'If I were in your red shoes, he would be gone by the end of the day. You have to set an example to all those staff below you — if you are caught stealing money from the business, you have to go. No second chances.'

'If I sack him,' she said, 'that could finish his career. Thirty thousand pounds seems a small price for the company. Do we really want to cast him on the slag heap for such a small sum? I'm sure a stern talking-to will be sufficient to put him back on the right course.'

'Bearing in my mind that my job has no limits on what are the sums involved in any frauds, I'm a little concerned,' I said, 'that such a crime should be missed by the auditors and yourself. OK, so we had a stroke of luck uncovering it, but someone — i.e. you, Ms Blair — didn't spot the higher level of bad debts and that something was amiss.'

'I keep myself focused on the bigger picture,' she said. 'Thirty grand is chicken feed. And, may I remind you, Shannon, that with Cooper gone, I am in effective control of the business. I call the shots now. I could get rid of you with one snap of my fingers.'

'It would look suspicious. That would probably kill your chances of getting any money from the NHS for the extension. Keeping me on board is your only chance of getting a cash injection.'

'Don't threaten me, Shannon,' she said. 'I eat people like you for breakfast.'

Palmer stepped in — bored by the technicalities, no doubt.

'Let's park the fraud for the moment,' he said. 'I have enough evidence to charge him if I feel like it. It would be good to keep on my side. Let's switch track. Can you tell me your movements on the afternoon of the day Cooper was poisoned? Let's start at one o'clock.'

She raised an eyebrow. 'You can't think I have anything to do with his death. Preposterous. What had I got to gain?'

'To return to my question, what were your movements on the afternoon that Cooper was murdered?'

'I was in my office all the time. Not all of the time, now I come to think of it. I did pop out for a sneaky fag — it's my secret vice. I didn't see anyone at that time when I went out. Rest of the time here, beavering away.'

'Can anyone vouch for that?' Palmer asked. 'Anyone see you on your coming and going for the sneaky fag? Anyone come into your office when you were beavering away?'

'I couldn't possibly say. You must know what it's like in a busy office, DCI Palmer. People just getting on with their working life. Other events don't impinge on what you're doing. No one can corroborate me being in my office that afternoon, and I couldn't alibi anyone either for that time. Blind alley, Chief Inspector.'

'As you say,' Palmer said, 'you are now in effective control. He who guards the money, calls the tune. I imagine you can veto anything you don't like by saying there isn't enough cash and, vice versa, saying you have enough money to support your recommended choice of action.'

'Any evidence to corroborate that theory?' she said. 'If you haven't, then I suggest you pick on someone else.'

'Why did you have lunch with Cooper last week?' he said.

She gave a jolt, sat back in her chair and stared at the ceiling. She would be trying to invent a plausible story on the hoof.

If she wanted to pull the wool over Palmer's eyes, she was going to have work hard. In his years on the force DCI Palmer had seen it all, more or less. Maybe death by morphine injection was a new one, but his instincts were still sharp.

'Last Tuesday, to be precise,' Palmer said. 'Who invited whom and what was discussed?'

'How did you get to know this?' she said. 'Have you been checking up on me?'

'This is a murder enquiry,' he said. 'To get to the truth, we have to gather every piece of evidence or we wouldn't be doing our job properly. So, I repeat the question: tell me what happened at lunch? We can easily do this back at the station, but that would indicate we have suspicions about you. We could even put the handcuffs on for dramatic effect as we lead you out past your employees.'

'There was nothing illicit in my relationship. We are both committed to our partners; we would not jeopardise those relationships. You can forget that line of enquiry.'

'I'll pursue that if it suits me,' said Palmer. 'Come to your home and interview your partner. Cast doubt in his or her mind. So, start talking. What was so important that the conversation couldn't occur in Cooper's quiet room?'

'It was nothing, really,' Blair said. 'He was getting cold feet about the extension. It was a lot of money. That bothered him. He wasn't a risk taker.'

My phone pinged. It was a text message from Norman saying to call him urgently. Work or home problem? Cherry? Is it time?

50

'One moment,' I said to Palmer. 'I'll be straight back.'

I walked out of the office and out of earshot. Called him with my heart thumping.

'I've got a result for you,' he said. 'The first thing I have to say is that no one seems to agree on the size of the market. Best estimate is around five hundred private hospitals and turnover in the last year of fourteen billion pounds — it's a big market, that's all they agree on. Valentine did some number crunching of forty rooms, average length of stay one week times average cost of treatment of fifteen thousand. It's a rough figure, but equates to the turnover of Fairstead in the last year. Now the interesting bit. The shareholders in Fairstead are Cooper, four consultants and Susan Blair. They all have a ten per cent stake in the company with the remaining forty per cent unissued. So, effectively, they own one sixth each. Makes for good dividends each year. Three million divided by six. Around half a million each.'

'Well done, Norman,' I said. 'While you're on, I was wondering how Cherry is?'

'Situation normal,' he said. 'So you can let out that sigh of relief. Things are a bit chaotic at the moment. I'll set you up a large vodka when you get back. Must go.'

I pondered for a moment — things chaotic. What did that mean? I walked back in Blair's office. 'What have I missed?'

Palmer turned towards me and said, 'The lady here says it was all about the extension. Was the allocation of space right? Enough medical, enough rooms for clients, enough scanners, enough theatre space, enough everything. The lady reckons he was getting cold feet? She soothed him by running through the numbers. Says she left him reassured.'

Blair nodded. 'That's about it,' she said. 'You can go and bother someone else.'

'Why didn't you tell me that you are a shareholder in Fairstead?' I said.

She paused, taken aback. 'I didn't see that it was relevant,' she said. 'I still have that opinion. This is quite common in private hospitals — one in six would be a good estimate — of consultants holding shares. Do some research and you'll find it to be true.'

'The new extension will either make you all very rich,' I said, 'or will ruin you. What side of the fence do you fall on? Presumably the former.'

'It will make us a lot of money,' she said. 'Cooper had nothing to worry about. He just needed a little reassurance. I ran him through the financial aspects and he relaxed. Sometimes it's tough being at the top of the tree.'

'Especially when Shannon is shaking it,' said Palmer.

Time for a different tack. Good cop.

'Susan,' I said, 'I'm not carrying out some sort of witch-hunt. I'm just here to see that nothing lurks under the surface — things like the credit control scam. I'm not against anybody in particular. Regard it as a simple chat with some interesting people and a final look through the accounts after the audit. I'm on a daily rate, granted, but that's no incentive for me to prolong it: there is plenty of other work in the pipeline. It's in my interest as well as yours to wrap this up quickly. So what corners are you cutting to increase the profits? It happens everywhere, so why should Fairstead be any different?'

'Hospitals are not like any other business,' she said. 'You're dealing with decisions and treatments that can make the difference between life and death. It's a pressurised environment. People deal with it every day in their own way. You'll find the best example of that when you interview the consultants. I won't spoil your fun.'

'That will be all for now,' Palmer said. 'Think again about the Jenkins business and what the effects will be on other staff if they were to hear about it.'

Blair nodded. 'You forgot the last order.'

'Which is?' Palmer asked.

'Don't leave the country,' she said.

* * *

'We need a plan of action,' Palmer said. 'I need to go back to base to oversee operations there. We've got initial statements from everyone here — frustratingly not worth the paper they're written on. I'm happy for you to continue interviews here providing you keep me abreast of any developments. Try to keep to the financial side and only bring in the murder when you sense something of interest. Then I can jump in. It's a strange role to play, you not being police, but anything you dig up here will be a benefit to you when your case comes up in court. Agreed?'

'I'll start with the consultants,' I said. 'This information about the shareholding changes everything. They're going to be very rich. Fairstead makes a big profit now — three million in the last financial year — distributing it via dividends — that makes the dividend worth around five hundred thousand pounds for each shareholder after paying off Cooper's share to his wife, I would presume. The new extension will be adding around a third in size. That's going to mean a quantum leap in profits — maybe around one and a half million pounds to be split among the shareholders. I never would have imagined that we would be talking those huge numbers. Gosh, this is one hell of a business. We are talking big money here. That could provide a motive for the murder if Cooper was getting cold feet and wanted to pull the plug, if you don't mind mixed metaphors.'

'I live and die by mixed metaphors,' Palmer said. 'Anyone outside these shareholders that would benefit from the extension? Anyone else you need to investigate?'

'The two account clerks, for sure. If I find any more frauds, they would provide motives, too.'

'Blair was pretty cool,' he said. 'You gave her a stumble when you said about the shareholding. Surely, she must have realised you would find out sooner or later.'

'It's a fine line,' I said. 'Technically, I'm only charged with finding out the profit and things that impinge on them. How they distribute those profits isn't in my remit. She doesn't know me and how I love to dig around.'

'Let's keep her as a suspect,' Palmer said. 'Motive. No alibi. Means — she would know where the morphine could be found and the antidote, too.'

'Time to let you go,' I said. 'You might even make your wife happy by arriving on time for a meal that hasn't been ruined by sitting around in the oven.'

'Depends what's in the office when I get there,' he said.

'Same for me,' I said. 'Check on how the troops are doing.'

And I wasn't prepared for what I'd find.

# CHAPTER SIX

I couldn't get through the door when I got back. I had to wait while four burly men said goodbye to Arthur. What the hell was going on? Did everyone need more protection? Was that it? My mind raced.

'At last,' Cherry said, when I stepped into the river room where everyone was gathered. 'What kept you?'

'The small matter of a murder, among other things,' I said.

'And have you made any progress?' Cherry asked.

'Not as such,' I said.

'By "not as such" do you mean none?' she said.

'Precisely.'

I walked to the drinks trolley and poured a large slug of vodka into a tumbler and added some orange juice, sipped with pleasure and sat down. There was a conspiratorial silence and all eyes were on me.

'What's going on?' I said.

'You'll find out,' said Arthur, smiling at some secret joke.

'What's new?' I said.

'I have a date,' said Anji. 'Well, not so much a date but an invitation. I have been asked to go out tomorrow night with Christine. It's to be a surprise, although she said it could be rewarding. She will pick me up at seven.'

'What else do you know?' I said.

'That's it,' Anji said. 'Anything else would spoil the surprise, Christine said.'

'Arthur?' I said.

'I'll cover Anji,' he said. 'Being reliant on this Christine woman for transport makes me edgy. Anji could be trapped somewhere.'

'What progress on Cooper's list?' I said. 'Managed to break the code yet?'

'We haven't found any links checking against the employee files,' said Valentine. 'There seems to be no direct link by role.'

'We've analysed the data every which way and nothing seems to make sense,' said Anji. 'We've sorted by job title, how long everyone has been there, salary, even alphabetical, but nothing jumps out. We need some sort of breakthrough.'

'Amen,' I said. 'Interesting development, though. Blair is not going to take any action on the credit control scam. Out of character. Too heartfelt. I'm looking for reasons.'

'Have we got her wrong?' Anji asked. 'Under normal circumstances, we would assume a relationship between her and Jenkins. Still possible, though. Are we displaying our inner prejudices?'

I took a long pull of my drink and looked out at the Thames steadily rolling by. So serene compared to the mess in which we usually found ourselves. Something about Cooper's code must make sense, if only we could find it. I raised an eyebrow at Cherry and Norman. They both nodded.

'Time for you and me to have a chat,' I said to Anji. 'Join me in my office.'

I walked through to my office and she followed me. We sat down at the conference table.

'Have I done something wrong?' she asked. 'This seems a bit like being called to the headmaster's study for a wigging.'

'You have nothing to worry about,' I said. 'On the contrary.' I paused for dramatic effect, just as they do on the television. Everyone loves good news. 'You'll soon have been with us for a year. Time to take stock.'

'Can I get myself a drink?' she said. 'This has all the hallmarks of something heavy.'

'Things are not always what they seem to be,' I said. 'I would have thought you would have learned that much after a year. No, you cannot get yourself a drink. You will sit silently while I say my piece and then you can get yourself a well-earned drink. As I said, you will soon have been here a year. You've made yourself a valuable asset. You have a bright enquiring mind and a sharp instinct on what is right and what is wrong. Things are slightly tricky because you don't have an official job title. We — Norman, Cherry and I — want to reward you. We want to give you a promotion. From tomorrow, you will move from no-job-title to one step higher. You will be an enhanced no-job-title. You will get a twenty per cent rise in salary. How does that sound?'

'You know,' she said, 'I'd work here for nothing. It's the best job there ever is. Thanks for all the good times. I'm thrilled and will carry out my duty as an enhanced no-job-title employee with pride. Do I get that drink now?'

'And a top-up for me would be good. Send in Valentine.'

'Your wish is my command,' she said.

Valentine entered, passed me a refill and I gestured for him to sit down at the conference table.

'Valentine,' I said.

'Yes?' he said, tremulously.

'You've been with us for six-months' probation, so it's time for reflection. You have done everything we have asked of you and done it excellently. You have an enquiring mind and a nose for anything suspicious. You have learned well and gained valuable experience. We have promoted Anji to enhanced no-job-title rank. As of tomorrow, you will be assistant enhanced no-job-title. You will have the same deal as when Anji joined. Your salary will now rise by fifty per cent to thirty-six grand. Keep learning, Valentine. Cheers. Well done. Let's go join the others.'

'Morag has cooked us all chicken in red wine with garlic mash and mange tout peas,' Cherry said. 'Why don't you go and change?'

'Excellent idea,' I said.

I climbed the stairs to the top floor. Opened the door and stood there aghast. The bedroom had disappeared!

In its place was all the furniture from our second-floor communal area. I raced down the stairs and entered the river room. 'What's going on?' I said, to faces unable to disguise their laughter.

Arthur piped up. 'Well, you can't expect Cherry to climb up all those stairs with two babies, so we moved your floor to the old communal area and moved that to the top floor.'

'Hence the four thugs,' I said.

'I wouldn't call them "thugs",' Arthur said.

'How about "quasi-thugs"?' I said.

'Sounds much better,' he said, 'although I'm not sure what "quasi" means.'

'There's still work to do,' Cherry said. 'Wardrobes need to be built — a man is coming tomorrow to measure up — and the small bedroom needs to be decorated and equipped for the babies. Exciting times.'

'I'll go and change and meet you in our new communal area,' I said. 'And you can wipe those smirks off your faces.'

Five minutes later, we were all seated at the table with the tantalising aroma of chicken in red wine on our plates.

'I didn't thank you earlier, Norman,' I said. 'Good work on identifying the shareholders.'

'Not as interesting as first seen,' he said. 'I've done more research. It's not unusual for consultants to be shareholders of private hospitals — around fourteen per cent have that sort of deal. The other wheeze is that a consultant buys equipment and charges the hospital every time it is used. So, can't make too much of it. I wonder what they will do with Cooper's shares? Offer a bargain-basement price to his widow and cancel the shares? That would make each of them having twenty per cent. There's so much money sloshing around that there has to be something in the hospital that's not entirely legal. My nose tells me there's some scam going on. All we can do is look with microscopic eyes at Cooper's computer files and the Fairstead accounts and hope something catches our eye.'

'I'll look at Cooper's files in the morning before I set off. The other lead, of course, is his phone. We're reliant on Palmer for that. Tomorrow is another day.'

And what a day it was.

# CHAPTER SEVEN

I got up at four o'clock. One of the side effects of the pregnancy was that when one of the twins kicked, Cherry kicked and the recipient of the kick was me. There seemed no point in lying there being woken up each time I dropped off and so I felt I might as well be doing something useful. I pulled on a dressing gown, made myself an espresso and sat at my conference table with its load of papers, my laptop, the Fairstead laptop and manila folders of HM records. It was a mess.

I fired up my laptop and inserted the memory stick that contained all of Cooper's files that we had downloaded. Palmer would like it — all the files were in neat folders labelled up for easy access. I went into Excel and examined what files were there. One was labelled *bank* so that seemed like as good a place as any to start.

The spreadsheet contained tabs for several accounts across four different banks. There was a mixture of the main current account, ISAs and investments. The figures confirmed what I had expected from the papers on his desk. He was solvent, highly so — well over a million — and his current account showed the dividends paid to him each year. He had no money worries apart from keeping track of everything. Nice problem to have.

The current account showed no deposits of cash or other funds apart from his generous monthly salary. He wasn't receiving unidentified credits. That ruled out him for blackmailing anybody unless there were off-shore bank accounts for ill-gotten gains and that was out of character. There were, however, large donations to several charities, including a local hospice and church, showing his Christian and socialist roots.

There was a spreadsheet called tax and I peeked at that. It contained details of his incomings and outgoings for tax purposes. The figures put aside for future tax matched one of the bank accounts. Prudent. No unwelcome surprise at the end of the tax year.

I made myself another coffee and started to feel more human. I went back to the filing cabinet icon and looked at the latest files in the list. No other spreadsheets looked promising, so I concentrated on Word files. The most recent file was only a week old and was with a firm of solicitors. It instructed them to call on the services of a barrister. Maddeningly, there was no earlier correspondence on the matter. I guessed that the first contact was probably via email or a telephone call. More digging needed. I wrote down the details of the solicitor in order to follow up later.

I then looked at his browser. His user name and password were auto populated, meaning these were filled in for me. Sloppy. There was a lot of spam, driven no doubt by a website or more that he had visited in regard to finance, suggesting he had money. Prime candidate. Had a target painted on his back. Recent emails were mostly conversations between friends and family and arrangements with partners for bridge.

Sites visited included comparisons for renewals for car, Audi 4 series, and house insurances. He must have been frugal with his money to consider comparing other firms to save a few pounds when he had all that money in the bank. I thought, *Life is too short*, and then tried to erase it from my brain, considering what circumstances had dealt to him. Not a good phrase to use.

There were many emails to the local church about bell ringing and other commitments. I was now getting quite a picture of the man he was. It made me sad.

I looked at my wonderful Cartier watch — courtesy of a well-satisfied client — and found it was eight o'clock. Four hours of detail after detail. I wrote a note to Anji and Valentine stating which files I had looked at and those on which they needed to concentrate.

I went back to our new floor, showered and shaved and then set off to Fairstead. I was handed a note at reception to inform me that an appointment had been made with the consultant on cosmetic surgery. I would be collected at the most appropriate time.

I immersed myself in looking more deeply in Fairstead accounts, specifically a deeper look at the income. Cosmetic surgery made up around forty per cent of the sales revenue which surprised me. How can a tummy tuck, facelift or Botox cost that much? Perhaps I would learn more once I had spoken to the consultant.

I was collected at ten o'clock by a lady about fifty wearing a dark blue nurse's uniform, including a white cap. She knocked at a door and immediately entered. Opposite a man in a three-piece suit sat a woman in her thirties. It was not what I expected.

'Sorry,' I said. 'I didn't know that you had a patient.'

'I thought it was time that you saw what happens at the coal face, Shannon. Come in and sit down.'

He, introducing himself as Gordon Owen, was aged around fifty-five and as far as I could see was dressed immaculately in a black three-piece suit. Under the suit was a clinically crisp white shirt and a dark blue tie. From under the sleeve of the jacket was a high-end gold watch, Rolex Submariner, and a pair of cufflinks with a lion's head enamel design. This was a man trumpeting his wealth and wanted the world to see it in no uncertain terms. His hair colour was irrelevant since he had none — his skull was bare and shaven, and shiny.

From my limited vantage point of the visitor's chair, I could only see the right-hand side of the woman's face.

'Well, Candice,' he said, 'tell Mr Shannon your story.'

'I was in a car accident,' she said. 'Another car going too fast and crashed straight into mine. My car caught fire and by the time I got out, I had third-degree burns.'

Owen interrupted and took a photo from a thick file before him. 'This is what happened to Candice.'

He passed me the photo. It showed Candice's face. The left side was obliterated by a purple ugly burn.

'Now turn to face Shannon,' he said.

She looked at me full face. There was no burn mark.

'Remarkable,' I said. 'This could be a different woman. How did you make the burns disappear?'

'You can go now, Candice,' he said. 'See you in a month for the usual check-up.'

She got up, smiled at me and left the room. I changed my seat to sit in the now-vacant chair opposite him.

'Most people think cosmetic surgery is about the vanity of a breast enlargement,' he said. 'What you have seen with Candice is what is called face reconstruction. I'm one of only three surgeons in the country who can work such miracles. It took a six-hour operation and multiple skin grafts to achieve what you have seen just now. Impressed, Shannon?'

'If there is a word for something greater than impressed, then I would use it,' I said. 'I hate to go for the vulgarity, but what did this treatment cost?'

'Nothing for Candice. The cost was borne by her insurance company. I think it was around fifty thousand pounds, if I remember rightly.' He made a gesture of inconsequence by waving his right hand in the air. 'May have been bigger. You tell me. You're one of the money men.'

'Such cases are rare, I expect,' I said. 'After that are we back to the breast enlargement stereotypes?'

'Oh, Shannon, why did you burst my bubble? Yes, the day jobs are the majority of the revenue we make but, every so often, there are cases like that of Candice. We rise to the challenge.'

'What do you make of the current circumstance, with regard to Cooper? I found the body, as you know, and am intrigued by what everybody was doing at that time. Could we have saved him if we had got help quicker.'

'I can tell why you got a reputation for digging deep. You're on a fishing trip, Shannon. All you really want to know is where I was during those missing hours when someone committed the deed. Sorry, but I was doing the equivalent of a ward round. A nurse will verify that. Afterwards I was here, updating the files. There's just too much paperwork. How can they expect me to do my job when I'm inundated with paperwork? Time sheets! You could look at those in connection to your task of money making. Personally, we all make them up.'

'Having worked out my hidden agenda, can anyone vouch that you were here?'

'I'll tell you what I told the police. I was diligently writing up the client files and had made it clear that I didn't want to be distracted. No. No one can alibi me.'

'How did you get on with Cooper apart from his love of paperwork and your disdain about it?'

'You keep loading that fishing line with bait and casting it in the middle of the river, don't you, Shannon?' he said. 'He was the man who was the vital cog in the machine but, as long as my monthly bill and annual dividend hit my bank account, I could tolerate him. He's going to be a hard man to replace. After the news reports, we have already had five enquiries about filling his boots. Just like the lawyers who follow an ambulance. Distasteful.'

'Where does the finance come from? How dependent are you on private treatments, as opposed to those paid by insurances in one way or another from the NHS?'

'Many of the more simple procedures are paid direct by the client. Boob jobs, facelifts, nose reductions and the like. Bread and butter, shall we say? Every day a silk purse from a sow's ear. The NHS is the jam on the bread. Operations on the obese or any of the backlog they can't do anything about. Fighting an unwinnable battle.'

'I only met Cooper once,' I said, 'but he seemed a likeable man. Was there a reality I had missed? Did he have any enemies?'

'Not that I would have guessed. He could be a bore when the subject was linked, however tenuously, to religion — Bible thumper. Convert the natives. But I can't think of anything that would warrant murder, unless you're a music fan and take offence at his poor guitar skills. Like a cat being strangled, it was.'

'I've heard about botched operations in overseas clinics. Does that boost business for you?'

'We pick up the debris,' he said. 'People don't seem to learn about value for money — "you get what you pay for" is my mantra. Can only blame themselves. But it's all grist to the mill. Time's up, Shannon. I've another client to see.'

'One last question, then,' I said. He sighed. 'I've heard a lot of talk about clients. No one seems to talk about patients. Why is that?'

'Because, at the end of the day, this is a glorified hotel. I'm sure some people invent a need, just so they can spend a fortnight in luxury here. Your time has now expired.'

He shook my hand, got up from his seat and opened the door. Not very subtle.

As I walked back to my allocated room, I made a mental note of the names on the doors. I felt the need to be able to find my own way round rather than being dependent on nurses and secretaries. As soon as I got back, I drew a map and, looking through the HR files, added the discipline of each consultant. It would also be of use if I needed to do any after-hours snooping.

I called Palmer to do a mutual update. 'What's new, Shannon?' he said.

'Working my way back through accounts and interviews,' I said. 'From what I can see, I don't think money was the motive for the murder for any of the consultants. All the consultants are loaded. They paid themselves dividends of half a million each in the last year. No wonder they want to get funding from the NHS — they basically clear all the profits in each tax year by paying dividends. The business has nothing to fall back on. We've not been able to find any code in Cooper's list of names, but we're still digging. No more anomalies in the accounts, but again, we haven't found any more frauds. From what I gather, Blair has decided not to punish Jenkins for the credit controller scam. Interesting. I can't think of any company who wouldn't have sacked him on the spot. Any developments your end?'

'Our boffins have run his phone through some black box thingy and unlocked it. Not much traffic on it. Mostly calls to his wife and tradesmen. More calls to a firm of accountants than we thought was usual at this stage of the tax year. Text to a Father John the day before the murder, requesting a meeting with him. I think you may get more from him than us. With us, he might clam up and plead the confidentiality of the confessional. You might be able to sweet-talk him. Want the details?'

I took down the address of the church and then gave Palmer a carrot to chew on.

'I've found an email with a firm of solicitors asking them to engage a barrister. I'll go and see them, if it's all right with you? You can come along if you like. No problem, but it might have nothing to do with his murder. Waste of time, maybe.'

'I think I'm more use here at the moment. Someone needs to keep control of the headless chickens. I've got fifteen officers in the team with no leads. If I'm not careful, they'll follow up and finish in dead ends. How are you doing with alibis?'

'I've only just started with the interviews, but no alibis as yet. I suspect no one can alibi anyone else. They're all busy people getting along with their solitary jobs. I'll keep pestering people and see if anyone breaks. What happened when you took your initial statements?'

'No joy. At least we've pinned down the time of the murder since finding the cassette player. Keep digging and we'll do the same. Keep me posted.'

'One last question.' I said. 'What details of Cooper's death did you reveal about how he died?'

'Just what you read in the papers,' he said. 'Murder rather than suicide.'

'I'll be in touch as soon as I have anything.' I said.

I went to find Christine and was ready to pursue the consultant in charge of hips and knees and to make some progress in any direction. I'd learned next to nothing from the interview with Owen, except that I thought he was arrogant and vain. Didn't make him a murderer, though. Or did it? So arrogant that he thought he could easily bypass the restrictions of the hospital with its closed environment. Would make for a good cosy crime murder. Those who are acquainted with the gods Hubris and Nemesis realise what would happen. Those that live by the sword die by the sword, that's what. Vanity would be his nemesis. I only hoped that I would be there when it happened.

The hips and knees consultant was called Barry Curnow and spoke with a Cornish drawl worthy of his name. He gave me a warm handshake and gestured me to sit down in his client chair around the L-shaped desk. Hell, even I was referring to 'clients' now.

He was short and tubby and was wearing a suit in a colour that fell into the taupe category which spanned the full spectrum of beige — take your pick. A plain white shirt and plain blue tie completed the ensemble. He had grey hair and eyes to match and a pair of rimless glasses. All in all, there was nothing about him to stand out from the crowd.

He spoke softly, and I had to crane forward in the chair to hear distinctly what he said.

'Thanks for making time to see me,' I said. 'Could we start with your background?'

'Nothing much to tell that's out of the ordinary,' he said. 'Medicine at Cambridge. Chose my speciality and started at the bottom of the NHS ladder working all hours that God sent. Climbed up the greasy pole from there. Been here for five years alongside my NHS work. All the rumours about doctors being paid a mint are completely untrue. If I wanted to have enough money for my dreams, I realised I would have to do private work. Added to that, I saw a lot of people in the NHS who deserved a pain-free life being held on waiting lists for a year or more. Life is frustrating — so many operations cancelled through malfunctions in the system. I get my job satisfaction here.'

'Things must be a bit unusual with Cooper's death and the new wing. It certainly shook me up. Finding his body and all that. Could have been anyone who found him, I suppose, but the bad luck came to me. What was the first you heard of it?'

'Not till I came in the next day and found the police here. I understand the murder took place in the afternoon. I had no need to see him during that time.'

'I guess the police have been checking alibis,' I said. 'Are you in the clear?'

'I'm not sure what time was poor Cooper's death, but I was in the operating theatre doing a hip replacement from three o'clock onwards.'

'And before that?'

'Getting ready for surgery,' he said. 'Here in this room, going through the client's notes. No one can vouch for me, I'm afraid. Still, I would have no motive for killing him. For killing anybody, I mean. Would be a foolish thing to do. For an operation, you need steady hands. If I had killed him, I'm sure my hands would be shaking like mad.'

Fair point. You'd have to be a cool customer to do that. And was he the kind of guy to commit murder? Didn't strike me as such, although you never know what goes through the mind of a murderer.

'How do you feel about the new extension?' I said, changing track.

'The extra operating theatre will be a boon. I'd not have to queue to do my job. There are so many people out there in chronic pain. I could work twenty-four hours a day and still not scratch the surface. Disheartening. Still, one does what one can, even if it's woefully inadequate.'

'How do you cope with the demands of the NHS and here in private practice?'

'One has to make a living,' he said. 'I couldn't have the lifestyle I want without working privately.'

'And what's the lifestyle?' I said.

'A few acres and a stately pile. It's a listed building going back centuries. You have no idea what a money pit it is. Outside here, I like the common pleasures of walking the dog and relaxing next to an open fire with a good book.'

'I see from the accounts the sheer size of the dividends that get paid each year. It seems to me that there is not much altruism here. Does that infringe any moral code you might have?'

'The way I look at it,' he said, 'if I didn't do it, then someone else would. Might as well be me, eh? But, Shannon, we seem to be drifting into philosophy rather than the job you are being paid for. Are you going to give us the all-clear?'

'I've found nothing so far that would go against you,' I said.

'I detect a *but* dangling in the air,' he said.

'But it's early days,' I said, 'and there's the complication of Cooper's murder. Will the ramifications of that go against you? Simple practices such as having the pharmacy store open for anyone to walk in and help themselves will count against you. You're going to have to sharpen up if you want money from the NHS. They'll want to cover themselves every which way.'

'I hadn't thought of that,' he said. 'Damned nuisance, Cooper getting murdered.'

'I'm not sure his wife would see it that way,' I said.

'I'm sorry,' he said. 'Didn't mean to be insensitive. Good place to stop, Shannon, before I put my foot in it again. We've both got work to do.'

I left him, hoping that our chat hadn't caused his hands to shake. Dreadful thought.

I had only the ophthalmologist and Ferguson to see from all the remaining shareholders and my trawl would be complete. I hadn't learned much so far, certainly not enough to rule someone out or, alternatively, put someone in the frame. I called the office and spoke initially to Beryl. I asked her how Cherry was doing this morning. Had she packed her bag yet? It had been something on our list of things to do for too long now. It came slightly below the injunction *Panic*. Beryl reassured me that there was nothing to worry about, and patched me through to Norman.

'Any progress?' I asked.

'We've got something of potential, but we'd like to do that in person. Don't want to go outside our group as yet. Might be building you up before letting you down. Arthur has got one of his mates painting the new nursery, so you don't have to worry about that. Remember that Anji is out tonight with Christine. Arthur is on standby, but it would be good to see you back here before she goes. Otherwise, situation normal.'

'That bad,' I said.

'Ha, ha. The good news is that we've had three new clients join the waiting list. I think news of the current job has leaked out. Must go — flat-pack cot to assemble.'

I decided on a walk around the grounds before Christine delivered my sandwich — corned beef with horseradish. And a pickled gherkin, of course. Can't have corned beef without a pickled gherkin. Uncivilised.

The car park had plenty of spaces and I looked first at those cars parked nearest to the building. Expensive. Consultants' cars. I tried to put cars to faces, or faces to car, if you want to look at it the other way round. There was a Range Rover which I put down to Curnow for all those icy times when delivering children to school. A Jaguar looked ostentatious enough for our cosmetic surgeon, Owen. An open-top BMW 5 series looked to have all the style for Ferguson, who I had yet to meet on business terms. I took a punt for the ophthalmologist and a safety-first Volvo. There was an Audi TT at the other end of the car park, but why park that far away from the entrance? You pays your money and takes your choice.

As I walked, I could see Arthur's white van. Always on duty. You can't do better than that. I was getting to the end of the grounds, just by a bricked-in area for rubbish and recycling, when I felt a presence behind me. I should have run. I stopped and turned.

The man was tall and muscled — spent too much time in the gym, evidently. He was wearing a hoody with his head covered and a balaclava for good measure. The most important part, though, was that he was carrying a curved sword like the Dothraki used in *Game of Thrones*. It was a slicing sword, because of the curve, rather than a sword made for stabbing. I guessed he wasn't there as part of a customer satisfaction survey.

I was in an exposed position, which was not good for defence. I needed to have something at my back to narrow down the points of attack. There was a covered area where all the waste and recycling bins were sited. If I could make it there, I would gain some time before Arthur saw what was happening and came to my rescue.

'You've been a naughty boy,' the man said, 'poking your nose where it shouldn't be. Time to teach you a lesson.'

I suppose I could have engaged in a debate about karma and what might happen to him if he persisted with his intentions, or what he might end up as when he was next reborn, but I decided that he might not be a philosopher willing to have a free-thinking discussion. I ran for the bin area.

By the time, he had registered what was happening, I had my back to the brick wall surrounding it on three sides. And I had several large bins in front of me. Armed to the teeth.

'There's no need for that kind of thing,' he said.

'Strange, but I was thinking just the same,' I said.

He raised the sword and drew closer.

I took hold of a black recycling bin and rammed him. He let out air as the bin hit his solar plexus.

'Don't make me mad,' he said. 'I'm dangerous when I'm mad. Let me just cut a hand off, and then we can both get on our way.'

'But that would leave me with only one hand,' I said. 'Could be a bit awkward for the rest of my life.'

'There is that,' he said, 'but life is never perfect.'

Maybe he was a philosopher after all.

I rammed him again. Hit him in the machete hand. He let out an expletive and swung at me again. I launched the bin at him and pulled another bin into play. I could now operate with two hands, repeatedly ramming him blow by blow, frustrating him every time he came forward.

I saw Arthur appear behind him.

'Can anyone join in?' he said.

'Choose your bin,' I said.

The man looked round to see who I was talking to. He gulped. Dropped the sword and held his arms in the air.

'You're Arthur "Dangerous" Duggan, aren't you?' the man said.

'I have that honour,' said Arthur. 'Not your lucky day, is it? Get down on the floor and stretch out your arms.'

The man complied.

'Sorry about this,' Arthur said, stamping a steel-capped boot on the man's right hand. There was a sickening crunch and cry of pain.

'We'll leave it at one,' Arthur said. 'A memento of our meeting.'

'Time to call Palmer and give him a present,' I said. I took out my phone and speed-dialled Palmer from the Favourites screen, even though the label didn't quite sum up our relationship. I could almost hear him rush out of the doors.

'If you don't mind me saying so, Arthur,' I said, 'you did cut it fine.'

'I'd been standing there for a while,' he said. 'You seemed to be managing well without me. I was always standing there waiting for how the fight might turn out. I liked the bin trick. Unconventional, but effective. I was always there ready to support you.'

'As ever,' I said.

'As ever,' he said.

'This remains with us,' I said. 'I don't want Cherry worrying.'

'And you don't want to drop the case, do you? God, you're a stubborn bastard at times, Nick.'

'I feel that I'm almost there,' I said. 'There's a break-through coming. Maybe this man will open up a new avenue.'

'Nothing to do with you wanting to complete the prom-ise you made when you took over the contract, then?'

'Promises should always be kept,' I said. 'Break a prom-ise and it's the start of a downhill slope.'

'What about your promise to Cherry that you would get out if things got out of hand? I'd call this out of hand.'

'There you've got me,' I said. 'I'd say that when prom-ises clash, you have to prioritise.'

'Sounds like a weasel,' he said.

'Maybe because it is,' I said. 'Between ourselves. OK?'

'As you wish.'

Palmer's car and a full-on police car with flashing lights and sirens screeched into the car park.

Palmer looked at us and surveyed the scene.

'Slipped on a bar of soap, did he, Arthur?' Palmer said.

'Lot of it going around,' said Arthur.

'You have two alternatives, Sonny Jim,' Palmer said to the man. 'Either we go to the police station and you sing as sweet as the birds in the trees or I walk on and leave you alone with these men. They can be very persuasive when they want. I don't fancy your chances of saving your other hand. Did you ever want to have children is a question you should ask yourself. They'd take your balls off with a cheese grater — long, painful and life-changing. The possibilities are endless.'

The man just lay there groaning.

'I'll take that as the station option,' Palmer said. 'OK, officers, take him away. Better ring the on-call doctor, but

we all know what the prognosis will be. Interview first, A &
E after.'

'How hopeful are you that he will give us some names
to follow?' I said to Palmer.

'Let's look at it this way,' he said. 'If you'd been engaged
to chop off somebody's hand, what's the likelihood of you
giving us a name?'

'Then you need to convince him that Arthur and I will
come after him and he'd lose those testicles after all,' I said.

'I'll bear it in mind,' he said. 'You must be getting close
to discovering something or why they are turning up the
heat. Any clues?'

'Norman said that they have something that looks fishy,
but I don't have any details. It may not be much, for he
would have told me more at the time otherwise, but it might
provide us with another avenue to follow. I've got two consultants and two account clerks I want to see and those will
be the final interviews, but Norman's lead might mean more.
As ever, I'll keep you posted.'

'I hope you'll turn up something or I may be in hot
water for giving you your head. My boss doesn't always like
initiative,' he said. 'Let's see what transpires with Dothraki
man. We may be lucky and he'll squeal like a pig. It's a funny
old world.'

'Amen,' I said.

\* \* \*

Arthur and I sat in the room sharing the corned beef and
horseradish sandwich I had ordered. I let him have the gherkin. That's friendship for you. The small room got even
smaller with Arthur inside. We were chewing the fat. We'd
finished our GOAT on an England football team and just
started with cricketers when Christine came in. Ferguson was
in town and had a free slot for me. Christine said his name
in awe and made me feel like I had just won the big prize in
the lottery.

Stuart Ferguson's consulting room was the same size as the others, there seeming to be no pecking order among the specialists. He stood up and shook my hand, gold blazer buttons catching the light, then settled back in his chair. He'd had a haircut since I had last seen him in the hospital, and the rugby player's cauliflower ear was more visible. Not a good move. Or maybe he was wearing it as a badge of pride.

'Just business this time,' he said.

'Almost,' I said. 'I don't know whether you were trying to minimise the potential anxiety for Cherry, who needs all the reassurance that's going at this moment, but should I be doing the worrying for her?'

'I'm trying to play safe,' he said. 'Not taking any chances. I'll treat her as a priority here. Get them to call me wherever I am when the time is near. There is the age factor, and the fact that it's twins has to be taken into account. Rest assured if complications come up, we'll be ready to take whatever actions are necessary. I'm just trying to cover all the angles. Relax.'

'Then on to business,' I said with a sigh of relief. 'A lot has happened since we last spoke, the least of which is Cooper's murder. Do you put anyone in the frame for that? Any rivalries here? Any enemies?'

'He wasn't the sort of man to make enemies,' Ferguson said. 'The Christian ethic, I suppose. High moral values. He was a man who would turn the other cheek to avoid any bad feeling. Unlike me, who can't suffer fools gladly, he had time for everybody whether they deserved it or not.'

'How close were you to him? Did he confide in you?'

'He kept his confessions, if he had any, to his priest. He and I weren't that close outside the business,' he said. 'It wasn't always the case that grudges would be kept, but there was some tension among us consultants that he should have an equal share of the business when it was us consultants making the money, but he did his job well. Pernickety at times, but he was the one to seek out if you wanted a moan. The listening ear, one could say.'

75

'The police have pinned down the time of the murder to around about two in the afternoon. Maybe a little earlier; they can't be sure. Have the police ruled you out? An alibi, in essence.'

'I had several clients to see in the afternoon before preparing for surgery in the evening. Christine can vouch for me, I would think. She seems to keep everyone under control.'

'So you were in this room the whole afternoon?'

'Apart from a comfort break, yes. Oh, I went to get a coffee around lunchtime when I had the opportunity to enjoy it. This does seem that we are straying away from your remit.'

'As I said, everything has changed with Cooper's murder. The business has lost its money man. That might worry the NHS. Will there be a vacuum, and how long will it take to fill it? Unknown replacement and unknown capabilities. Not good as the start of a relationship.'

'There are lots of people who would give their eye-teeth to work here. As ever, there's reassurance to be done. That's what a doctor should be good at.'

'Whose idea was the extension?' I said.

'No one in particular,' he said. 'It just occurred because we thought we could do so much more if we had more space. Recruiting the staff would be easy — we have a good reputation and pay well. Nurses would be queueing up for a chance to work here. Somehow the idea just took wings. I don't know how it started, but everyone agreed that it made sense. I'd like to claim the idea for myself, but it probably started with a drink in a pub after work.'

I knew how he felt — sometimes the downtime is the most fertile. The river room was our equivalent of the pub.

'How much of the time is taken up by caesareans? I said.

'Around one in eight births nowadays is by C-section,' he said. 'It's got more popular over recent years. It makes for an easy birth and suits a lot of women who want to avoid the hours spent in pain for an unaided birth or, simply, to recover their body shape sooner. But it's not all about C-sections. The majority of my time is spent on the preparations for birth. You've seen it yourself — the regular scans and suchlike. Plus, the calmness of reassurance.'

'What happened with your surgery session?' I said.

'Went ahead as normal,' he replied. 'Didn't make much sense to cancel. The show must go on. Isn't that what they say?'

'So is it just about the money?' I said. 'Or how much is altruism?'

'You've seen the figures,' he said. 'You've seen how much is the figure for dividends. We are all well off — millionaires, all of us, multi-millionaires. We don't need more money, although the increased payout will go down well in my pension fund.'

'They say that murder is either about sex or money,' I said. 'If we eliminate money, what are we left with?'

'He wasn't the type for extramarital affairs,' he said. 'So we draw a blank. You have three more questions and then we call it a day. First question?'

'How familiar are you with the pharmacy?'

'Could I have helped myself to morphine, you mean? Like everyone here, I have access if one of the nurses isn't there and there's an urgent need. I can administer an injection — child's play for all of us here. Next question?'

'When is the last time you would use a scalpel?'

'When do I plan to retire, you mean? You do have a roundabout way of asking questions, Shannon. I could retire now if I wanted, but I'll keep serving the sick for a few more years yet. Last question?'

'What is the question I should have asked?'

'You'll never know.'

Don't bank on it, Buster.

* * *

I never did understand eye specialists, optician, ophthalmologist, optometrist. Let's call her ophthalmologist. Her name was Deborah — 'call me Debbie' — Caxton. She stood about six foot in her stilettos and was wearing a denim jumpsuit

— I wouldn't have guessed it, this was a consultant after all. Her hair was blonde and had a fringe Claudia style. There would no argument that she was attractive — not beautiful like Cherry, but looks that could attract a man. She welcomed me with a smile and a warm handshake. There was a gold ring on her left hand and a heart tattoo on her left wrist. Interesting.

I guessed her age as just below forty, although it was difficult to be exact nowadays, with facelifts and Botox and the like. I wondered what Gordon Owen, our resident cosmetic surgeon, would do to her if given a chance. Nothing, I hoped. Whatever he might do would end up looking unnatural, out of my presumed character for her. She looked like she would be fun for a night in the pub drinking prosecco.

Her room was the same size as that of the other consultants, but had a machine that projected rows of letters, diminishing as you read down. Standard eye-test fashion. In addition to her L-shape desk, a frightening piece of machinery on wheels stood ready to examine eyes closely.

'What can I do for you?' she said.

Sounded like we would get off to a good start.

'As you know, my remit here is to authorise the business with five stars so the NHS could feel comfortable with their investment. That remit evolved into something bigger, a whole different beast, with Alan Cooper's death. You must trust me when I seem to be going off-piste.'

I liked that — off-piste — I made a resolution to use it more.

'So what do you want to know? How off-piste are you going to be?'

'I have to feel satisfied that Cooper's death won't affect the running of the business, so let's start there. What was the first time you heard of it?'

'I'd taken the afternoon off — needed to buy something special for a new date. Don't look judgemental; my husband died of cancer three years into our marriage and I now use the phrase *carpe diem*, live every day — so the first I knew was the following morning when the police were swarming around.'

'What time did you leave?' I said.

'Just before two, as soon as my last client was gone. I was running behind time — as do all doctors and consultants — so it was nearly two before I was able to get away.'

'Can anyone confirm that?' I said.

'Do I have an alibi, you mean? You might add left-field to off-piste. I was having a sneaky fag in the car park before leaving. I've got a brand new Audi TT Roadster parked as far away from other vehicles as possible and don't want the inside polluted by cigarette smoke. If someone was walking back to here, they might have noticed me. I saw the police car, lights flashing, siren blaring as I drove away.'

'How did you get on with Cooper?'

'Do I have a motive? Is that what you mean?' she said. 'You are so much fun, Shannon. I'm enjoying this. You don't happen to be single, by any chance?'

'Wife about to have twins.'

'Isn't that always the way? Well, I'll put you on reserve when the nights are broken and not by anything to stir your loins. Where were we? Motive, that was it. Cooper was a likeable guy, but a bit of a proselytiser. Bible thumper, if you gave him a chance: we were all agreed on that. We got along fine. Why shouldn't we? We were all making shedloads of money. Why would we want to upset the lucrative status quo? Doesn't make sense. Next question, Shannon baby?'

'I don't know much about what you do. Might Cooper have had any enemies?'

'What I do is examine the patient's eye for problems — that's what you get with an eye test with an optometrist — such as glaucoma and cataracts and do surgery when necessary. Much of my work is done through referrals from opticians and personal recommendation. The problems can be huge or as vain as someone wanting contact lenses to change their eye colour — blue being most popular,' she said. 'Moving on. Did anyone have a grudge big enough to kill him? Not that I'm aware. Certainly not here. He could be a pedant at times, but he was in control. He was the one always looking after the business. From what I know about the fine detail of finance, he was clever enough to save us a fortune in tax. No, I'd look outside for your quest for a murderer.'

'What do you know about his death?'

'Obviously murder, by the persistence of the police, but no more than that. That cop called Palmer is a strange one — at one point, he leaned over and rearranged the pens on my desk. Anyway, the strategy should be to get on with our jobs till the speculation dies down. Forget about "in the billiard room with the candlestick".'

'Was there any tension around the shares being divided equally? Did any one of you think that was unfair?'

'Nothing I know. We all make oodles of money with the current shareholding. Too much hassle to change it. We'd probably spend weeks agreeing on a new formula. We all play a valuable role in the business. There's cross-fertilisation that happens: my eye patients might choose to have their hips done here and vice versa.'

'How will the new extension affect you?'

'The extension will boost work all round, but less so for me — my patients rarely need an overnight stay, so the effect on me will be minimal. Are you sure you're not in the market for a little fling?'

'I believe in honour,' I said. 'I made some vows at our wedding and I'll never break them, but thanks for the flattery.'

'Well, no harm in asking.'

'Where are you fishing at the moment?' I said.

'A bit of online dating, and men often come to talk to me when I'm in a bar with some girlfriends.'

'You're too nice and bubbly to be on your own for long,' I said. 'Hang on in there.'

I stood up. The interview could stop here. I was sure she wouldn't mind me coming back for more.

'Time for me to go,' I said. 'You can kiss me on the cheek, if you like.'

'Rotten flirt, Shannon,' she said. And then that's what she did.

# CHAPTER EIGHT

I got back to Docklands at five o'clock, my head spinning with ideas. I'd spent the last half hour trying to book an appointment with Prendergast, the hospital's solicitor. He, Michael Prendergast, saw no point meeting me as Cooper was dead, and as far as he was concerned, any details would now be with Blair until a new CEO was hired. I started talking about referring everything I knew to the police. That would be far more disruptive than an hour spent with me. He finally gave me an eleven o'clock slot the next day — if I would pay the hourly fee. I made a resolution to report Prendergast to Palmer for anything I could think of once I had sucked him dry. Sweet victory.

I called everyone into my office and we sat around the conference table. I updated them on the happenings that day — minus Dothraki man, of course — and asked what progress they had made.

'We have two new areas to have a look at,' said Cherry. 'Let's start with the easy one. Anji, report.'

'It may not be anything,' she said, 'but we delved deep into the purchases. One company gets a hell of a lot of spend. I think someone said they award a lot of contracts to the lowest bidder via tenders with sealed bids. It seems odd that that business — Ampard — is so luckily low that they so often win the tender process. A bit too coincidental.'

'We thought it might be good,' said Valentine, 'to know about who is involved at Fairstead and how the process works.'

'Are we all thinking the same?' I asked.

'Someone is fiddling the bids,' said Norman. 'Leaking information on the bids received and allowing Ampard to come in cheaper than the rest at the last moment. Simple scam.'

'Only three people could have done it,' I said. 'Blair, but why would she do it when she's loaded? Too risky for too small a reward — which I suppose doesn't rule out doing it for fun or the joy of beating the system, but I'm not buying it. Which leaves one or both the account clerks that I am yet to meet. I'll add that to tomorrow's to-do list. How to prove it could be a problem, though, but worth a try. Right, what's your second possible scam?'

'It's not so much a scam,' Valentine said, 'but interesting. There are a lot of foreign names on the sales ledger. Names with lots of consonants and few vowels. We can't quite work out why. Do they have someone in Albania, for instance, who touts for business for them? It just seems odd.'

'Follow up on the foreign names — money spent, procedure or treatment,' I said. 'What do we get on the purchase ledger? Any payments to foreign-sounding names or businesses who are based overseas? Any large payments in cash?'

'Not as we noticed,' said Anji, 'but we weren't looking at those specific areas at the time. We'll check tomorrow. I hate to mention it, Nick, but I need to get changed. Christine is picking me up at seven and I don't have a clue what to wear.'

'Tricky,' said Cherry. 'Could be a blind date' — Valentine frowned — 'in which case you need to dress up. Could it be something more business-like? What do you do with your hair — scraped back and sophisticated, or go for a more seductive looks with flowing hair?'

'I don't like this,' I said. 'Why be so secretive about where you might be going? Arthur will be back-up for you, but I want to know everything that goes on right down to the last detail. You won't be able to take down notes without it becoming suspicious. You're going to have to commit everything to memory. Which means if there's drink involved, you need to keep sober and look out for anyone who might spike it. As I say, I don't like it. At the merest sign of danger, you call Arthur and get out of there.'

'I have to drop in at Toddy's tonight,' Norman said. Toddy's was the restaurant he owned and managed by head chef — Toddy, obviously — who was the chief cook at Chelmsford prison. It had a reputation for great ingredients, local whenever possible, cooked simply so that the tastes shone through. It was hugely popular and tables were booked a month in advance. How he got to own the restaurant is another tale, but involved his normal financial chicanery. 'I thought I'd treat Morag to dinner. It's been a while since we went out together, just the two of us. We won't be late back. I don't want to miss a thing.'

'I'll hang around,' said Valentine. 'Just for support and in case I might be needed. I can start some trawling through the accounts — checking the things we've just decided.'

'I'll go and change for dinner,' said Morag.

'I'll get some drinks,' said Beryl. 'River room?'

'Excellent idea,' I said. 'Vodka and orange juice now, and then no more alcohol until Anji gets back.'

Everyone drifted through to the river room and I hung back with Cherry.

'How are you doing today?' I asked.

'Situation normal,' she said, 'if you could call carrying twins and worrying about a C-section normal.'

'I don't think you need to worry. I talked to Ferguson and he said he was just covering all the angles, not taking any chances. You couldn't have a more qualified person looking after you. It'll all work out fine. Trust me.'

'How are you progressing about your promised deadline?'

'I'd like an extra day or two,' I said. 'I was a bit optimistic as to when I would be finished.'

'You want to renegotiate the deal, don't you?' she said. 'I can tell.'

'Just another day or two, that's all.'

'I'll go along with that on one condition.'

'And that is?'

'I want you to meet with Johnny Silver. You're going to have to trust me for a change. I'll send you all the information I have on him. He's only in London for a couple of days each month for board meetings and such. Book something before he goes back to his Caribbean paradise. On second thoughts, I'll book it. I don't want you to renege on the deal a second time.'

'River room,' I said.

I took her by the hand, kissed her on the cheek and led her through.

* * *

Anji had decided on something middle-of-the-road for her evening. She wore a dark blue skirt two inches above the knee with a pale blue top and silver pumps: good choice — you can run faster in pumps.

She got back at half ten with Arthur hot on her heels. 'Drink,' she declared.

'Ditto,' said Arthur.

I poured a white wine for Anji and took an ice-cold beer out of the fridge for Arthur.

Valentine immediately came from my office where he had been working and poured himself a low-alcohol cider.

'Spill the beans,' I said to Anji. 'Every detail.'

'Let the girl have a sip of her drink first,' said Arthur. 'I'll fill in for a while. Christine May had a small grey Fiat 500, five years old judging by the plate, and led us to a hotel near the City Airport. She was dressed businesslike, black trouser suit and white blouse. I followed them inside and saw a notice board with those white letters you push into grooves. There was only one meeting booked. Same organisation.

Each night this week. No others to complicate things. The company name was Sweet Look. Could have been anything. OK, Anji, take over.'

'It was a large room with capacity of about seventy or so, set up with long tables seating around six each,' Anji said. 'There was a raised platform where one man and a woman stood. They had a presentation to make. I could see that there was a memory stick slotted into the projector. The first slide was projected on a large screen. It just had the Sweet Look logo and a line which read "Your chance to get rich". Christine got all excited, like she was feeding off the tension. It was like some religious cult.'

Anji took a drink of her wine and looked up at the ceiling as if all the details were written there.

'The presentation took about forty minutes, after which I was hoping to go, but the two people on the stage circulated and we all sat there waiting for our turn for a hard sell.'

'What was the deal?' I said. I pretty much knew what was going to happen, but it had to be confirmed.

'The big deal was that the audience consisted of investors like Christine and trapped punters like me. That's why she had picked me up and driven me there — there was no way out. The crunch? For an initial fee of a thousand pounds each of us would get a starter pack of Sweet Look toiletries and cosmetics to sell, but the big money was to be gained by recruiting others to work under you. For each new investor recruited, you would receive a hundred pounds. However, once you had recruited five people you could double your investment and earn two hundred pounds per new recruit. The presentation showed quotes from satisfied investors and the amount of earnings was backed up by redacted bank statements. Christine showed me a copy of her latest statement which showed the credit of a hundred pounds. She was delighted — she'd made ten per cent in a little over two weeks. Come aboard, Anji girl! This is your chance to get rich.'

'Valentine,' I said, 'while Anji enjoys her drink, go on to Wikipedia and search Ponzi Scheme.'

'Classic,' said Norman. 'I didn't know that scam still existed.'

'I only had three cases in all my time at the Fraud Squad,' said Cherry. 'Like Norman, I thought it had gone out of fashion. The problem is that by the time the scam is discovered, the people at the top have cleared out their bank account and done a runner. Everyone else, like Christine, loses everything they've paid in.'

I topped up Anji's wine and poured a vodka and some ice cubes into my orange juice. Cherry shook her head — she had no enthusiasm for drinks anymore. Everything tasted bland to her. It wasn't as if she could go back to alcohol after giving birth — twins to breast feed. Small price to pay, but that was me talking.

'Tell us what you've learned,' I said to Valentine. 'What's the essence of the scam?'

'Robbing Peter to pay Paul,' he said. 'One of the frauds is similar to pyramid selling.'

'Good work,' I said. 'Here it is in more detail. The original fraud was pulled back in the ninetieth century and revived by the eponymous Charles Ponzi back in 1920. Initially, the mechanism deployed high-interest bonds, but it's been used many times for a bunch of cheap products where the sale of the products is immaterial. This is how it applies to Christine. She, the punter, is lured into a thousand-pound investment. The punter has to believe that each recruit will give him or her a hundred pounds, a very good return on the investment in such a short time. The fraudster pays the hundred pounds out from the thousand-pound investment of another recruit. He pockets ninety pounds from the transaction. And so it goes on until there are no more victims to attract, and then it folds and they make a run for it.'

'Clever,' said Anji. 'What are we going to do?'

'You and Valentine are going to construct a presentation. More details before I go in the morning. See if Sweet Look has a web page. We want a logo; the rest is immaterial. Anji, call Christine and tell her you were so impressed that you want to come along tomorrow and that I and Valentine want to invest, too. We dangle the fly before the fish.'

'I think we should let the Fraud Squad know what's happening,' Cherry said. 'We might be able to freeze their bank account and impound any other assets. Get a little back for those who have been swindled.'

'Get a couple of them lined up to join us tomorrow,' I said. 'Be good to deliver it to them on a plate. Put us in good odour if we need a favour, too. And, Valentine, call your dad and tell him we've got a scoop. Right. Busy. Busy. We've all got a big day ahead of us. Time for bed, Florence.'

# CHAPTER NINE

I was working in the small office at the hospital when Palmer showed up bright and breezy at ten o'clock. His shirt was without a single crease and the handkerchief in the top pocket of his jacket was at a precise angle so that it was a perfectly aligned pyramid triangle. I wondered how long it took him to dress in the morning.

So far, I had yet to find any evidence of the fraud involving what we were certain was going on in the background with Ampard. I might have to wing it and hope that the account clerks would put their hands up in a simple manoeuvre of surrender. I didn't fancy my chances of overcoming a series of 'no comments'.

'What's new?' Palmer said, rearranging my desktop. 'How can you work in such mess?'

I ignored him and hoped he could focus on the murder.

'What's new?' I said. 'I was just about to ask you that,'

'It's too early in the day to go into banter mode, Shannon. Spare me the wit and answer my question. Let's try again: what's new?'

'There's another scam going on, but I suspect it will be petty, and not of a magnitude warranting murder. There's also a pyramid selling con that I'm hopeful will be shut down tonight. We've got the Fraud Squad coming to the big unveiling, but you could tag along if you like. Could be fun.'

'Any relevance to the murder of Cooper?'

'No, even though his PA, Christine, is one of those about to lose money they can ill afford. Innocent victim, unfortunately. Now, your turn. What's new at your end?'

'We've run up against a brick wall,' Palmer said. 'To recap, we've cracked the code of his mobile by running it through some wizardry black box or other, but nothing of interest. We suspect he wasn't a heavy user. No frequent calls to any paramours so we can rule out a passionate affair. He wasn't short of money — you found that out. Millionaire a few times over, in fact.'

'How about his widow?' I said. 'Did she come up with anything that might suggest a motive and be worth following up?'

'Big fat zero,' he said. 'He was squeaky clean. I suspect his strong Christian faith meant he would do no wrong. Wouldn't cheat on his wife, for sure. Wouldn't be a part of anything illegal. I can't see anything remotely guilty in his behaviour. What did he know that would justify his murder?'

'I've got interviews with his solicitor and with his priest, today,' I said. 'If I find out anything useful, I'll let you know straight away and you can do formal interviews. There is one other thing we're investigating. It may be nothing, but when looking at the sales side of the business, there are lots of what I think are Eastern European names.'

'Does that suggest a possible scam?' Palmer said.

'Not that I can see, but we'll carry on digging and hope that something turns up,' I said. 'As you know, my methods are to shake the tree and see what falls down.'

'A lot of that going on,' he said. 'What about the share-holders? Anyone remotely suspicious?'

'Not at the moment,' I said, 'but there's one consultant I hope is guilty. Nothing to back that up.'

'Is it worth us doing a bit of surveillance?' he said.

'It's hard to tell what might be achieved by that,' I said. 'We know they are loaded, so a Porsche in the driveway doesn't prove they're living above their earnings and need a bit of cash now and again. There's the prospect of adding fifty per cent to their earnings, too, with the new extension. Someone doesn't like me digging around, so there must be something they don't want me finding out There has to be something hidden away and there will be a connection to Cooper's murder. I just wish something jumped out. I've got both Anji and Valentine working all the time to dig around.'

'What about Cooper's coded sheet? Made any progress with that?'

'We've looked at it all the ways possible, but we still don't have a clue. What about Dothraki man — anything you learned from him?'

'Just "no comment" over and over again. There'll be a hotshot lawyer soon and they'll get him off through something technical that we haven't done and get him free. We could lock him in a room with Arthur and wait for him to surrender, but we're not allowed such things nowadays. Pity. Many a case has been solved that way.'

'I'll forget you said that,' I said, 'but I go along with your feelings.'

'I knew you'd say that,' he said. 'Back to reality and your precarious position re the trial. I'm working on a mitigation defence, suggesting how hard you have worked with us and the crimes we have solved through you. I except I might get a bit emotional, but that will be useful in its own right. Hard to know how well that will go down with the jury, but can't do any harm. You've pleaded guilty, so it's all about the length of sentence. I'd hate to see you having to go back to prison, but everyone is doing their best.'

'Keep my pecker up, eh,' I said. 'Hard to see anything else. It won't be good to miss the twins' early development. I'm trying to block it out of my mind. Cases like this are a boon. Enough. Hey, Palmer, want a coffee?'

He looked over the desktop.

'Only if there's a drip mat involved,' he said.

'Some things never change,' I said.

* * *

The two accounts clerks lived in an office only big enough to accommodate two desks, two seats behind the desks and two high-back chairs for times when they had guests, which I guessed would be unlikely. Their jobs didn't generate many avenues outside small talk. Query over expenses about the only time and that would be a pointless experience. I picked up a chair, turned it around so as to get that classic pose where my arms were on top of the chair back and placed it in between them and prepared for a verbal tennis match.

There was a classic pinboard to which were pinned holiday postcards from the heights of the Caribbean to those from a holiday park in Clacton. I wondered where they were on the spectrum.

There was one woman and one man, both conservatively dressed, mid-fifties and unremarkable. Strange to think that this pair was the engine room of the business.

'Tell me about Ampard?' I said.

The man spoke first. I saw a bluff coming. He wasn't going to succeed. Done too much of it in my time. Talking to an expert.

'One of our best suppliers,' he said. 'PPE, furniture for the office and for client rooms. It goes on and on. Dependable and cheap. Quality good, too.'

'Now tell me how the bidding process goes for tenders?' I said.

The man went shaky. The colour of his skin went pale as blood drained from him. The woman came into the rescue. She was going to fail, too.

'We prepare the document with what we need from the supplier, add on any conditions like date of delivery, penalties when things go wrong, that sort of thing and send that to three suppliers. Lowest price wins. Simple as that. We've been running that for years. If it works, don't fix it, isn't that what the Japanese say?'

'You've both been here how long?' I said.

'Three years for me,' the woman — Cathy — said, 'and two for Brendan. It's a good place to work.'

'Was a good place,' I said. 'but we'll park that for a while. Who goes through the tenders when the documents come in? How do they come in?'

'Mostly they are emails,' the woman. 'Copies for each of us. We look at the numbers and award to the cheapest. Process over without a hitch.'

'The tender documents are in what form?'

'Mostly pdf. Ampard is in Word.'

'Is the Word document enabled for editing? I can check, so don't try to pull the wool over my tired eyes.'

'Yes,' said the man, recovering his vocal balance from their muted mode. 'But that's not relevant.'

'It must have been easy money with low risk of discovery,' I said.

'I don't know what you mean,' the woman said.

'Simple. You open the two tenders from other suppliers, look at their prices and type in a new figure for Ampard's Word document,' I said. 'The only questions are how long it's been going on and how much does Ampard pay you.'

'I don't know what you mean,' she said.

I sighed.

'Tell him, Cathy,' the man said. 'You're better at words than me. He knows. Why else is he here?'

'You're right, Shannon,' Cathy said. 'Hands up. We've been doctoring the tenders. It's like you said. We edit the page that has the tender price. Little harm in it. We only take ten per cent and the business is still getting the lowest price as if it was when looking at the other two selling prices.'

'How long has this been going on?' I said.

'For the two years Brendan has been here,' she said. 'It was his idea.'

'Don't put all the blame on me,' Brendan said. 'You didn't take much persuading. You could have vetoed the suggestion and reported me to Blair.'

'What were the mechanics of the deal? How did it start?' I said.

'The sales manager took us to lunch because we were good buyers and as a welcome for Brendan. It sort of built from there. Maybe too much wine, maybe the sales manager sensed something in us. There was the germ of an idea blossoming. Brendan broached the subject, dropped it casually into the conversation. Then the only thing left to do was agreeing the figure.'

'How much have you skimmed?' I said. 'I can check on the accounts and come up with a figure, but that would be tedious.'

'Only about twenty thousand each.'

Chicken feed in the overall business. No wonder it didn't ring alarm bells.

'And how much can you pay back?' I said.

'We spent the money by building an extension downstairs for our son,' said Cathy. 'He has muscular dystrophy and is virtually wheelchair bound. We built a bedroom for him with an en suite, and widened entry to some of the rooms downstairs.'

*Hellfire.* The story resonated with me because of the death of my sister when I assisted her suicide and found myself spending seven years in prison.

'And what about you, Brendan? Have you got a sob story, too?'

'You have to understand, Shannon,' he said, 'that these aren't high-paying salaries. Cathy and I jog along, no more.'

'Do I have to repeat the question?' I said. 'How much have you got left?'

'Very little,' he said. 'I took the family to Disney in Florida. We haven't had a proper holiday in years. At least I'll have those memories with me when I do my spell in prison.'

I swore inside, upping *hellfire* to something unprintable.

'You're going to have to leave me with it while I work out what to do,' I said.

I rose from the table and, no longer Mister Cool, put the chair back in its original place. I walked out of the office with the strains of 'He Ain't Heavy, He's My Brother' ringing in my ears.

\* \* \*

I suppose they could be brothers, but my appointment with Prendergast & Prendergast was with Michael Prendergast, who was around thirty-five. I put him down as son. Time would tell.

The reception area was in a building from an era of two centuries past and was stuffy and claustrophobic. Little air circulated and what remained seemed to be sucked up by excessive brown furniture. I pitied the elderly lady at the reception who had to sit there day in and day out breathing in nothing.

'Nick Shannon,' I said. 'I have an appointment with Michael Prendergast at eleven o'clock.'

She scuffled through the papers on her desk — and there were plenty — and smiled at me. I wondered how many clients she had each day. How much relief from the tedium?

'I've been told to tell you that Young Mister Michael has another appointment at eleven thirty.'

She pressed a button on the telephone and both of us waited.

'Nice job, is it?' I said, to kill time.

'It pays the bills,' she candidly said, before lowering her gaze to something more important and resuming typing.

Maybe she would be at the stage of not minding if she had to move on or not. I wondered how many people in the building felt the same way. A few minutes later, a middle-aged lady dressed formally with white blouse over a dark green tartan skirt came to my rescue. She was called Irene Clancy and announced herself as PA to the aforesaid Michael

— or Young Mister Michael, as he seemed to be called by staff. She led me through a Dickensian landscape to an office on the ground floor where Mr P. was sitting behind a huge partners' desk with the sun directly behind him and, thus, straight in my eyes. If it had been my office I would have turned the desk around and looked out of the window with blinds when there was any glare.

He was dressed in a brown tweed hacking jacket with leather over the elbows. About to saddle up for a hunt. His hair was immaculately cut and came from an epoch where short back and sides was different from the Peaky Blinders cult in fashion now. I made the introduction and waited with bated breath.

'You know that I don't need to see you or answer any questions,' he said.

Good start.

'I understand exactly what you mean,' I said, 'but this is a murder enquiry and boundaries need to be widened. There is evidence that could be useful in the pursuit of the enquiries relating to Cooper's death.' I paused so as to build the tension. 'I'm working with the police in helping to solve this murder. If at any stage I think you are being obstructive, I only have to refer yourself and your staff to the police. The offices here could be closed down as a crime scene. They'll take every file out of the building and scatter them all around. They will disrupt your work for about a week. Maybe two. Do we understand each other?'

'Perfectly,' he said, 'although you must recognise that we are solicitors. We can take various measures to frustrate the police.'

'Do you really want to see your name in the papers? Go viral on social media, which I think you have no clue about?' I said. 'What's the problem with talking to me for half an hour about the affairs of a dead man?'

'I do not like to be intimidated.'

'Neither do I,' I said. 'It's going to be a hard-fought battle. That's if you go down that route. What would your clients think when they learn you are frustrating the police in a murder enquiry? Hardly good PR. Shall we start again?'

He nodded. It would have been so much easier if he had rolled over earlier.

'When did you last see Cooper?' I said.

'About two years ago.' Prendergast said. 'There was little to do for them. Nothing legal in the business that required attention.'

'And yet he sent you an email about instructing a barrister. There must have been something big brewing. What was behind that decision?'

'He wanted to dissolve the business. Wind it up and start again with new shareholders. I thought it was economic suicide and told him so. How would the business operate under a new structure? Where is the money coming from without the consultants? And what about the image of the company? It speaks of a big problem behind the surface. Skeletons in the cupboard.'

That would seem to account for the more frequent meetings with the accountant. Another box ticked in the puzzle.

'What was behind all this?' I said. 'Something profound, it must be. What did you know of the rationale of what triggered his thinking?'

'All I knew was that he had lost faith in the consultants. Wanted a clean sheet. Start again with a new team.'

'What else did he say?' I said. 'What was behind such a drastic move?'

'He didn't say. He said that it was a long story and he'd tell us everything when we briefed a barrister, which is not cheap. I would have guessed that the problem was that he only owned a sixth of the shares and the consultants could gang together and have him voted out. Suicide again, I told him. Digging his own grave.'

'And yet he wanted to go through with that,' I said. 'Can you think of any legal circumstances he might be able to push through his plan?'

'Gross negligence would be the most likely reason,' he said. 'Unless there was something illegal going on, but what did he have to prove his course of action? Frustrating. I wish I had phoned him to talk it through rather than relying on wretched emails.'

'Do you know whether he had raised matters internally? Had a chat with a consultant or two. Tried to sort something out with anyone?'

'It was supposed to be a highly secret matter. Only us and the barrister would know what had happened to provoke such a course of action.' He looked at his watch. 'I think your time is up, Shannon. There is nothing else you can suck from me. If anything comes up, I'll let you know. Goodbye. I wish I could say it's been a pleasure.'

Me, too.

* * *

I drove back home and mulled things over while doing so. Prendergast had confirmed my gut feel that something big was going down. I was no further ahead as to what that was. Maybe if I followed in Cooper's footsteps I would uncover what that was. Maybe.

Anji and Valentine were working at my conference table, searching for what they did not know. I debriefed them on what I had learned, which was not much, so didn't take long.

I changed tack. 'What progress have you made on the Sweet Look logo?'

'All done,' Anji said. 'We just need to know from you what to add to create the sideshow.'

'I only need three slides and might not use them all,' I said. 'Just make them look credible, as if nothing has changed. It has to be a shock after the first slide.'

I dictated what to put on them and said to copy them as a presentation on to a memory stick. It was going to be fun tonight but, unfortunately, not for the investors — they should at least get some of their money back if we had acted fast enough.

'As for the hospital, let's research more,' I said. 'Delve into the foreign names you spotted. Try to see what they were in for, who was the consultant and how much they paid. We're after any pattern.'

I wished them good luck and headed off to see Father John. The church was in Islington, only a short walk from Cooper's home. There was a parking space outside the church and I grabbed it thankfully. It was an affluent area and should provide plenty of donations each Sunday. I estimated that it was a couple of centuries old and would be worth a mint if ever it got planning permission to convert it into apartments.

There was no one in the church apart from a figure kneeling down in front of the altar with his back to me. On hearing my footsteps on the granite floor, the figure got up and turned towards me. He had on a pair of grey slacks, a loose black sweater and the white collar of the priesthood. The full regalia was reserved for formal occasions, I guessed. He smiled at me. Always a good start. Be positive, Shannon. This could all be informative, if you hit the right nerve.

I introduced myself and my mission. He didn't blink and pull down the shutters.

'I don't know how I can help,' he said. 'Alan was a great supporter of the church. I was shocked when I heard of his death. I don't know why someone might want to kill him. Come into the vestry and I'll make us a cup of tea and we can talk without fear of being overheard.'

We walked into a small side room where I could see his vestments hanging up — hence, the vestry, I suppose. It was a cramped room that wouldn't have seen many visitors. There was a wooden table just big enough for four at a pinch, but only two chairs. A sink was in front of a window looking out over the graveyard and he filled a kettle and set it on a gas stove. 'Tea?' he said.

I nodded. 'I see from Alan Cooper's notes that he arranged an appointment with you last week. I'm working alongside the police. Can you tell me what it was about?'

'He telephoned me — always considerate. Never just turned up.'

'Like me?' I said.

'Like you,' he said. 'Don't let it bother you. My door is always open.'

'That's what Cooper used to say.'

'As I said, a considerate man.'

The kettle whistled and he poured a little boiling water into a brown teapot, as if his mind was elsewhere, swirled it round and tipped it down the sink. He completed the laborious process by adding tea — three spoonfuls, remembering one for the plot! It was displacement activity. He was distracting himself from a conversation he didn't want to have but found inevitable. He poured me a cup and we sat opposite each other at the table.

'He was troubled,' Father John said. 'He wanted to talk about right and wrong. Doing the right thing for the wrong reasons and vice versa. He was a moral person and could not handle conflict or self-doubt.'

'That is my feeling, too, from the little I knew of him,' I said. 'Did you find out anything concrete behind his thinking?' I said. 'How much did he reveal?'

'He talked about losing his faith,' he said. 'How he was a money lender in the temple of Jerusalem. How money could corrupt. How, sometimes, a person has to stand up for what is right, even though there were bad consequences. I thought he probably knew what path to take and wanted reassurance that he was doing the right thing. I got the impression that his course of action was like ripples spreading out across the still waters of a lake. It would have major repercussions, some incalculable.'

'Did he leave you with any feeling that he had been reassured?' I said. 'That any doubts in his mind had been resolved?'

'I think the talk with me was like catharsis for him. The spilling out of the course of action he had to take. I take no credit for that. I was just the person that acted as a sounding board. I got the impression that he hadn't confided in his wife, that he didn't want to burden her. There was no one but me to act as a mentor. He was alone in his quest to find the true reason between right and wrong. That's all I can tell you.'

'Let's continue on the topic of right and wrong. I have a decision to make. Shall I do right for the wrong reasons or the other way round?'

'Oh, I think you know the answer to that without my views,' he said. 'Take courage, my son. It is time to act.'

I shook his hand and exited through the heavy vestry door.

I drove back, my mind set.

* * *

There was a sense of gloom pervading the air in the accounts office. Cathy and Brendan were looking up from the computer screens to the ceiling where they sought divine inspiration. They'd have to settle for me.

I picked up a chair — not trying to be Mister Cool this time — and placed it the right way down so I could look easily at both of them.

'I have a deal for you,' I said. 'Take it or leave it. If you leave it, I report you to Blair and also to the Fraud Squad, in which we have many friends willing to pick up where I have started. You will both go to prison — not many years, but enough to complicate your lives both present and future.'

Brendan said nothing, and I could see tears forming in Cathy's eyes.

'Tell us the deal,' she said. 'Not that it will not make a difference to the way I feel. I'll agree to anything.'

'Stand up,' I said.

They stood up from their chairs. I cast an eye over them. Brendan had a middle-age spread and Cathy was pear-shaped.

'You'll do, but it will take time to get you in a condition for the challenge,' I said. 'This is the deal. You both enter for the next year's London Marathon. Ampard will sponsor you to the tune of twenty thousand pounds each — if they don't, I'll report them for fraud. The money raised will be given to charity — Muscular Dystrophy UK. You will pledge not to do anything like this ever again. How does that strike you?'

'I'll go along with that,' Brendan said. 'As Cathy said, I'd go along with anything.'

'And you, Cathy? How does that take you?'

'You have a deal,' she said, 'although I don't know how I'll do.'

'It's the doing that is important,' I said, 'and the pledge. I'm a man of honour. I rate promises undertaken as unbreakable. If you renege on your pledges, I will punish you harshly. Right. One of you get me an espresso and let's talk about business.'

Brendan returned with the coffee I needed as an antidote to Father John's builders' tea. I waited while he sat down, until I had their full attention and could start my questioning.

'Let's start with Cooper's murder,' I said. 'Where were you in the afternoon it occurred, say between one o'clock and two?'

'We were both here beavering away,' Cathy said. 'Heads down. We ate our sandwiches as usual — Christine brought them into us — tuna mayo for me and cheese and pickle for Brendan. We chatted for a while.'

'About what?' I said.

'Holidays mainly. Would Brendan go back to Disney with kids? Too expensive. Maybe an all-inclusive in Egypt or Turkey? What would the food be like? Cheap buffets with the Germans swooping?'

'Cathy said her choice was non-existent — that she would never be able to go on holiday again,' said Brendan. 'We were a bit silent after that. In answer to the hidden question, we both alibi each other, although whether that will satisfy the police . . .'

'Did anyone come here during those critical times?' I said.

'You draw a blank there, too,' Brendan said. 'No one can alibi the pair of us together.'

'Does either of you know how to use a syringe?'

'We're bookkeepers,' Cathy said, 'not nurses. I wouldn't know one end of a syringe from the other.'

'Same for me,' Brendan said. 'Worse, in fact. I don't like needles.'

'Let's get technical,' I said. 'You're the engine room of the business. Tell me what feelings you have about the accounts? Does anything seem odd to you?'

'Some of the sums involved are staggering,' Cathy said. 'It's not unusual for treatments of fifty thousand or more to be involved. Mainly cosmetic surgery.'

'And,' Brendan said, 'keeping track of the detail is a problem.'

'In what way?' I said.

'Paid through a bank in Switzerland,' he said. 'Paid in euros, which means we have to convert to pounds. What conversion rate do you take? It's a bit like licking your finger and sticking it in the air. We usually wait to see how much hits our British bank account. Delays are never good when you're trying to keep track of the latest figures.'

'Is it just that one account paying the bills?' I said.

Cathy nodded. 'I'll let you have the details, although you can see for yourself by looking at our sales ledger.'

She was right. We'd missed that. Sloppy work by us. No, make that me. I should have thought of that.

'Anything else?' I asked.

'There's the cash receipts, too,' Cathy said. 'We both go to the bank to pay it in. Could be ten thousand or more at a time. Makes us feel uneasy till it's paid in. Should really have a courier company to do that side of things. It's not fair to put the burden on us.'

'Is that it?' I said.

They looked at each other and nodded.

'If anything else comes up, phone me,' I said.

I gave the pair of them my business cards and walked out of the office. Time for fun. At last.

\* \* \*

I gathered the troops in the river room and ran again through the plan for the evening. Everybody groaned at the repetition, but I'd rather overkill than leave something to chance or poor memory. Everybody, thus, knew their part and it involved a bit of luck and a fair level of chicanery. Valentine and Anji were to accompany me and Arthur would stay at the wharf and look over the others. Two members from the Fraud Squad had confirmed their attendance and that they had done what we had asked.

The room was exactly how Anji had described it. What a girl. There were three short steps up to the stage where the presentation would be given. I could see the control mechanism for the projector with its memory stick. People were beginning to gather and I saw Christine near the middle of the stalls guarding a table for six. She kissed me on the cheek and shook hands with Valentine. Anji got a hug.

'This is so exciting,' she said. She did that trippy-trappy dance with her feet that some women do naturally when greeting an old friend.

We sat down and waited.

Two people, a man and a woman both smartly dressed — the same two as before, I took it — appeared from the curtain on the left wing. Now was the moment.

Anji got up. She took a bottle of water from her bag, took off the lid and passed it to me. Together we walked down the aisle and up the steps. I smiled broadly so that they wouldn't be worried and held both arms spread wide in a non-threatening gesture. We moved across the stage and Anji stopped near the projector.

'Such an honour to meet you,' I said. 'You've made such a difference to our lives.'

As I was about to shake hands, I lost my grip on the water.

'So very sorry,' I said. 'Clumsy me.'

We looked down on the floor of the stage and the water had spread wide. I made a fuss of trying to mop it up with a tissue. I had their full attention. Anji coughed, giving the signal. I apologised again, stood up and went across the stage and down the steps. Anji was at the bottom waiting for me. Mission accomplished, we took our seats. As I sat down, I noticed two men in suits sitting at the back of the room. One of them gave me a wink. Fraud Squad had arrived: either that or I'd made a new friend.

The lights dimmed. The man on the stage walked into a spotlight and picked up the remote control for the projector. The first slide reassured them.

Anji had said that neither of the pair had 'startled rabbit' syndrome where the presenter keeps looking behind him at the screen in panic fearing that the right slide wasn't up there.

Anji and Valentine had done a good job. The Sweet Look logo looked perfect and the strapline of 'Your chance to get rich' was just as intended. It was the second slide where the fun would start. 'You've been filched', it said. Lower down was a bullet point: 'It was all a scam'. There was a hush from the audience as the reality of it sunk in. The two Fraud Squad officers walked up the aisle. I followed them. As the two presenters were arrested and handcuffs applied, I moved to the microphone.

'Let me explain,' I said. 'You've been scammed into what is called pyramid selling. Here's how it works. The fraudsters — the two people who have just been arrested — take your thousand pounds and put it in their back pocket. The thousand pounds from the next recruit is split into two parts — nine hundred pounds is pocketed and a hundred goes to you to keep you sweet and feeling great that you've had a very good result from their investment. Sooner or later, there aren't any new recruits and the fraudsters do a runner with their pockets bulging. The good news is that we have managed to freeze their bank account and we hope we can recover some of your losses. Give your contact details and size of your investment to the Fraud Squad officers, and we'll start the process of trying to get some money back.'

I walked back to my seat and saw that Christine was in tears.

'I worked hard for that money,' she said, 'and now I've lost it. What a fool I've been. A fool and his money are easily parted. Isn't that what they say?'

Anji hugged her, trying to be some sort of comfort.

'We'll try and get back whatever we can,' I said. 'How much depends exactly on how clever they have been and where else they have been pulling the scam — this won't be the only place, I reckon. Is the account frozen the only one, or do they have several? How much has been salted away where we might be unable to find it — accounts offshore, for example? It all may take some time, but rest assured, we're on the case.'

I walked across to one of the Fraud Squad officers.

'Neat trick, Shannon,' he said.

'Thanks for your support,' I said.

'Anything for Cherry,' he said. 'Give her my regards. How's she doing?'

'Edgy,' I said. 'We're close to the due date. I'm edgy, too, to be honest. We're all trying to occupy ourselves with mundane things to stop thinking about it. Not always successfully.'

'I've been there,' he said. 'It can be a dark place. I suggest you keep her sober while you get drunk. Frequently.'

'Best bit of advice I've had yet,' I said.

'Don't forget it,' he said.

# CHAPTER TEN

'We need a break,' I said to the crew on Friday morning.' We've been too close to see the wood from the trees. We've missed things — the cash, for example. We'll recap today and move on again. I'm to blame for not getting a focus on the problems. Norman, how about we go to Toddy's this evening. Clear our heads for a while?'

'Sounds like a plan,' he said. 'Table for eight at eight. Leave it with me.'

'Tasks,' I said. 'Anji, continue to look at the foreign names. I want everything. Consultant, operation, how much, how they paid and anything else that comes up from the results of your trawling.

'Valentine,' I said. 'Keep focusing on Cooper's list. Find a link. If necessary, go through everything a second time.

'Cherry. Can you check what the competition are charging and, if you can, how they are rated for service? Strengths and weaknesses.'

'And what are you going to do?' she said.

'I'm off to Fairstead Hospital to shake as many trees as I can. Watch this space.'

\* \* \*

Susan Blair wasn't delighted to see me. She cooled a little when I said I would only be another few days. All I wanted from her was an update. She didn't kick me out — which was progress. Her muddy-brown eyes looked at me with contempt. Her pixie-cut hair seemed more like an imp today or a gnome, perhaps. Too much hair gel to keep it in place — nothing moved when she turned her head. I hoped I'd found her before she was distracted by the urgent need for a cigarette.

'What's new?' I said. 'Anybody who might fit into Cooper's shoes?'

'What do you think I am, Shannon? A magician who can conjure a replacement out of thin air? Somebody itching to take over the spot of a murdered man? Wise up, Shannon. It's going to be a long haul, although I do have one idea that might solve things swiftly.'

'Your colleague, Mister Owen, told me you'd already had five people enquiring about Cooper's job. What has changed since I spoke with him?'

'Underqualified, some of them, and the rest want a shareholding that we are not prepared to give at this time.'

'You do appreciate that will influence my recommendation in the final report? Anything you think will mitigate that decision?'

'Only the fact that we are a tight management group that can cover the disturbance of the loss of Cooper. We can hold the fort.'

'I've noticed you have a lot of foreign patients,' I said. 'How did you manage that?'

'Word of mouth,' she said. 'One satisfied client from abroad who sings our praises and the floodgates open. Good business maxim.'

'I follow the same rule,' I said.

'But you have to kill someone to get your message across,' she said.

'That might be the same case here, for all I know.'

'There is no one here that is a murderer,' she said.

'Someone had to do it,' I said. 'Why not you, for instance?'

'Because I never left my office the whole afternoon, apart from a few minutes to have a sneaky fag.'

'As alibis go, it's a bit flaky,' I said. 'No one can vouch for where you were when he was killed.'

'I'm just not the type,' she said. 'I couldn't murder anyone. I cried for a week after I had to have my cat put down.'

'Anyone can murder,' I said, 'given the right circumstances.'

'And what might be my circumstances?' she said.

'DCI Palmer says it's always about sex or money. Either of those ring any bells?'

'I certainly didn't have a sexual relationship with Cooper, and I have all the money I need. Rules me out, then, eh?'

'Who benefits from Cooper's death?' I said.

'Just complicates matters,' she said. 'No one's after his job, so that makes theories about dead man's shoes invalid. I doubt that any of us would have a clue at what he did. Way above us, certainly. All his death achieves is uncertainty. Who would want that?'

'It seems to me that someone doesn't want me digging around,' I said. 'What's the skeleton in the cupboard? What is it that someone doesn't want me to find out? What was it that Cooper had to die for?'

'Just a fantasy, Shannon,' she said. 'You've got a vivid imagination. Maybe someone had a grudge against him. Simple as that. No skeletons in the cupboard.' She smiled. The sort of smile that a crocodile makes just before it eats you. 'We should be friends. Stop these verbal tennis rallies that serve no purpose. Let's work together to achieve that higher goal. Let's get on with our jobs. How does that sound?'

'A dream,' I said. 'Let's just keep out of each other's way. Soon it will all be over. Thanks for your time,' I said.

'Just remember I made this offer, Shannon,' she said. 'I gave you a choice and you turned it down. I hope you live to regret it.'

I stood up, nodded and walked out of the office. I would seek more fertile ground. *Yah, boo sucks, Blair.*

\* \* \*

The warmest reaction to me over the course of my interviews had been from the flirtatious ophthalmologist, Debbie Caxton. It would be good to rule her out of the murder and eliminate her from hiding a secret, whatever that might be.

She was wearing a black leather skirt two inches above her knees and a silk blouse in white. Her heels were high and made a statement: what it was I did not know, except that no one could put her into a stereotype. She wore the shoes better than Blair — more natural. Her startling blue eyes roamed over me and she smiled.

'Thought you'd finished with me, Shannon,' she said 'An unexpected treat. To what do I have this pleasure?'

'Before I get on to the main event, I have one question.'

'Fire away,' she said.

'Are your eyes naturally that colour, or do you wear coloured contact lenses? Forgive me, but that's the way my mind works.'

'They're fake,' she said, 'but I'm flattered you noticed. I have a couple of other colours, too. One black — mysterious — and the other brown — reflective. You'd be surprised what a difference a colour makes. My natural colour is grey — too boring. Are you still wedded to the expectant mother?'

'Yep!'

'Well, you haven't finished the job yet. Still time. I won't give up hope.'

'What did you buy for your date when Cooper was murdered?' I said.

'Business, business, Shannon,' she said. 'Always business with you. If you must know I bought a pair of denim dungarees to wear over a pale blue top and black ankle boots with killer heels. Casual all the way. *Tres chic.*'

'Did you hear Cooper's guitar when you were leaving?' I said.

'What a strange question,' she said. 'Now I come to think about it, yes I did. That must put me in the clear. He must have still been alive when I left.'

'Maybe,' I said, not wanting to tell her about the cassette player that was integral to the murder. You never know. The murderer might trip him or herself up by revealing critical information that only they could know. 'Has there been any friction about the equal shares when the source of the revenue was so skewed? Didn't reflect the worth of the business generated by each consultant.'

'If that was true, I would be a minority shareholder,' she said.

'Exactly,' I said. 'What will happen to Cooper's shares now that he's dead? Divided up equally, or a reason to reassess the shareholding? To change the status quo?'

'Interesting,' she said. 'I hadn't thought of that. Let's wait until Cooper is buried before we get into unseemly squabbles, please. So undignified.'

'Did you see Blair outside smoking a cigarette when you left?' I said.

'Can't say I did,' she said, 'although I might have been distracted by my own longing for one.'

'Out of interest,' I said, 'do you declare on dating sites that you're a smoker?'

'You've got me there,' she said. 'Hands up. No, I don't. I know I should be honest, but I don't want to narrow the field. Plenty of time to 'fess up if the relationship goes anywhere. Look, I'm having a barbecue tonight — a few friends, people from here. A chance to relax for the start of the weekend. Why not come along? See what we're all like in an informal setting? And, before you reveal yourself as a chauvinist, women can barbecue.'

'Prior engagement,' I said. 'Time to treat the team to dinner before a weekend of work. I value team spirit highly. Any other time would be great.'

'Don't tell me,' she said. 'You'd bring Little Miss Pregnant along.'

'I wouldn't put it quite that way,' I said — God, Cherry would scratch her eyes out if she heard that — 'but yes, I'd bring her along.'

'What else have you still got to do here?' she said. 'When is it you start to hand your role as inquisitor over to the rightful owners of the police? I'm the only person to like your company. Time to call it a day before there is open rebellion.'

'There's usually a *but* that follows that sort of statement,' I said. 'It implies *or else*.'

'Time for us to part, Shannon,' she said. 'It might surprise you, but I have an operation to do — cataracts — and I need to prepare. Come back and join me for a coffee sometime. Till then it's *au revoir*.'

'Just before then,' I said. 'How much would you benefit from the new extension?'

'There would be more slots for operations,' she said. 'It would speed up how many procedures I could do, but the effects on me would be minimal, no more. I'd be richer, but how rich do you have to be to love life? *Hasta la vista*, Shannon, baby.'

I blew her a kiss and left her to her own devices, whatever they might be. I wondered if she was playing too soft, too easy, too desperate, in the quest for the new partner in her life. Playing hard to get might be a better strategy. I would leave that advice to the next time we met, but wished she had some luck in the meantime.

I went back to my allocated office and sat there pondering. Christine, still with little to occupy herself, I guessed, came in and asked if I wanted to have a coffee, and what was today's sandwich order? Yes to the first question; roast beef with horseradish again on white to her second. She brought me the coffee and stood there for a moment.

'Can I interrupt?' she said.

'Pleased do,' I said. 'Get yourself a coffee and take a seat.'

She disappeared and returned after a minute or two.

'Still finding time can drag?' I asked.

'Gives me too great an opportunity to think about what a fool I was over being sucked in the pyramid thing,' she said, 'and then that it might have been worse. I could well have

111

scratched enough more money and paid another thousand to move up a level.'

'Don't beat yourself up,' I said. 'You could see how many people were there and fell for the same scam. You're not the first and won't be the last. These scammers are professionals: they spin a good yarn. What's it done to your finances? Are you strapped for cash? I could sort you out a loan if you need one.'

'Why would you do that?' she said.

'Because you're a good person and I would hate to see you suffer. Plus the fact that you're not going to flee the country, right?'

'We'll get by,' she said. 'We pretty much live close to the edge financially. Have a staycation this year instead of foreign climes. Tighten the belt for a while.'

'Well, the offer is still there if you change your mind,' I said.

'How much longer are you going to be here?' she said. 'I'll miss you when you're gone.'

'And everybody else will breathe a sigh of relief,' I said.

'No one seems to like you,' she said. 'Does that not bother you?'

'I do have one friend here — Debbie Caxton — but you're right about the others. It's a cross I have to bear. Couldn't do my job without ruffling a few feathers. I find people can open up when they're defensive. Little bits of truth can drip out of the falsehood.'

The door opened. Blair came in, and I could see she wasn't pleased to find Christine there.

'Haven't you got anything better to do apart from chatting to Shannon?' she said.

Christine placed her half-drunk coffee on the desk and slunk, chastened, out of the door.

'Contrary to what I said earlier,' Blair said, 'I've got the perfect replacement for Cooper. Woman I knew a few years ago before I came here. She can start immediately. Here's her CV. Put that in your final report.'

'And smoke it?' I said.

'Don't tempt me,' she said. 'I can find other ways for telling you where to put it.'

She slammed the door as she went out. Petty.

I sought out Christine and asked her to get me fifteen minutes with Gordon Owen, the cosmetic surgeon. My record for annoying people in the morning was high, so why not add another to the list? Then I waited for a reply. Positive, hopefully. But what were the odds for that?

The sandwich arrived with Christine and the news that Owen would give me fifteen minutes, no more, at two o'clock. She was conscious of the fact that Blair didn't like her talking to me, so left immediately. I told her not to forget about my offer — goodness knows what Blair would make of that.

I phoned Valentine and asked him to send me a scan of Cooper's list. An idea was forming.

Two o'clock came, and I knocked on Owen's door and entered. He had his jacket off and hung on a hanger on a hook on his door. No creases. The Rolex and cufflinks were on full show. Who the hell wears cufflinks nowadays? Today's pair were gold around blue enamel matching Caxton's eyes. I had to admit they had a certain style.

'Still fishing, Shannon?' he said.

'Still waiting for something to take the bait,' I said, 'but I don't give up easily.'

'Well, dangle away. You'll soon be gone, and uncertainty will be gone with it. How far are you before your report is done and you can get out of our lives? That's the only reason for me to see you. Plus I enjoy our little sessions.'

'Another couple of days; just a few more pieces to slot in the jigsaw.'

'Had to switch metaphors, eh, Shannon? I must be winning our skirmishes.'

'Tell me about Spanish guitar music? A fan?'

'I'm not uncouth,' he said, 'but there's only so much I can stand. I like something a little bit jollier. Some lyrics, too, would be good.'

'Middle of the road?'

'Never middle for me in anything. Only ever the top.'

'The choice of a Rolex isn't very adventurous. You could have chosen something more individual from Switzerland for the money, more of a statement — but let's go back to Spanish guitar music. Did you hear anything playing from Cooper's room that lunchtime?'

'Thankfully not — he wasn't much good, to be honest. We humoured him. As I told you at our first truth-or-dare joust, I was in here typing up some notes. Any music would not have come this far.'

'Tell me,' I said, 'How much morphine does it take to kill a man?'

'Morphine, you say?' he said. 'That confirms the rumours. The police have been cagey about how he was killed, but then it's the deed rather than the means that matters. I think it would be at least three syringes, but would have to take account of factors such as weight of the person to be killed, and things like other drugs being taken. Not a bad way to go. Painless, obviously. The victim would just slip away. A peaceful death.'

'Maybe that makes the killer a thoughtful person. Assuages the guilt.'

'As you say,' he said. 'Better news now, though. I hear that Susan has found a replacement as the successor to Cooper. Last link in the jigsaw, as you said. No reason now not to give us a clean bill of health in the eyes of the NHS. A good metaphor in the circumstances, don't you think?'

'I wonder how much of the new extension is about greed rather than alleviating the pain of patients,' I said. 'Would Cooper have been happy with that, given his Christian principles?'

'Please don't add religion to the argument; that would just cloud matters. Time to go, Shannon,' he said. 'Talks of philosophy bore me. Please exit before I start to yawn.'

'Many thanks,' I said. 'Most enlightening.'

'Shut the door on the way out.'

I went back to my allocated office and thought deeply for a while. Was the picture becoming clearer, or had another dimension been added? I was optimistic for the first time in the contract. After weekend working, I reckoned I could draft the report. I walked out of the building with a spring in my step.

\* \* \*

We had a drink in the river room before we set off for Toddy's. The Thames was serene as I stood gazing out over the jetty. How lucky we were. I debriefed everyone, and we were no further on finding answers to our questions, apart from an inkling in my brain. Let it stay there and grow to fruition. We were fairly confident that there were no other scams happening in Fairstead. After reading the CV of the replacement to Cooper, I had to agree that she seemed a sound candidate. If Cooper had not been murdered, I would have been able to pass Fairstead with a clean bill of health. Big if. I had another look at Cooper's cryptic list and smiled.

Dinner at Toddy's should provide a break from all the detailed work we had been putting in. A breath of fresh air to blow away the cobwebs. Our taxis arrived and we finished our drinks and set off.

The restaurant was fully booked as usual and there was a happy buzz in the air. It was smiles all round. It was almost inevitable, I had found, that in a restaurant there would always be one couple arguing. Not at Toddy's. Impossible. The vibes are against that.

The walls were duck-egg blue and table linen in navy blue. Tableware was chunky and helped with the solidity of the ambience. Our waiter acknowledged Norman with deference and took our drinks order.

We studied the menu of the day and chose from the meat and fish options. I was not feeling adventurous, so went for a rib eye steak. Rare, with chunky chips — never fries at Toddy's — and a side salad. Arthur had the same:

dependable decision. Norman chose a bottle of pomerol and asked for it to be opened to breathe. Cherry pushed the boat out with an order of fizzy mineral water with a slice of lemon. I had heard something about pregnant women being able to have the odd glass of wine, but we were not prepared to take even the slightest risk. The twins were too important for that.

I was conflicted — half of me wanted to discuss Fairstead and the other half to give everyone a break from business. I decided to go with the flow. I wondered if Valentine had seen the answer to Cooper's code. Would he have reached the same conclusion as me? He was good and ripe for learning — a great attitude. Anji, sitting next to him, touched his hand at times as if it was the most natural thing to do.

'Well,' said Norman, 'shall we get rid of the elephant in the room? Fairstead.'

'What is our strength?' I said.

'We're good at what we do,' said Anji. 'That makes us strong. We have yet to find someone to beat us.'

'The words are "we" and "us",' I said. 'What do we learn from that? Valentine?'

'We are stronger because we are a team,' he said.

'And Cooper's code?' I said to him.

'Nothing makes sense,' he said. 'I've looked at it every which way. Linkages by job title, function, specialism, whatever. There is no common factor. I don't get it.'

'Wind back,' I said. 'What makes us stronger?'

'That we are a team. We do different jobs, but there is something that binds us. I repeat, I just can't figure it out.'

Anji took him by the hand. 'Yes, you can.'

She had got it.

Valentine took a sip of his cider and stared at the ceiling.

'That's it,' he said triumphantly. 'We are a team. The people with ticks are a team. They all have different jobs, but work as one unit. They are a team.'

'I think the ones with ticks are the team he was sure about,' I said. 'The ones with question marks are those he couldn't be sure about. Our priority must be the team with ticks.'

'What binds them together?' I said.

'Let me have a go?' Anji said. 'They all have a function to do. If you wanted to do something illicit, you need the whole team working with you. So it's surgery. That would need everyone to pull together.'

'And so,' I said. 'What type of surgery do they do?'

'Everything,' said Valentine disconsolately. 'Cosmetic surgery seems the likeliest candidate, I suppose.'

'So where does that lead us?' I said.

'Find out what they're doing,' Valentine said.

'Exactly,' I said. 'Starters arriving. We can make that work tomorrow. Time to talk about cricket.'

'Not that,' said Cherry. 'Not again.'

'You can learn a lot about cricket,' I said. 'Teamwork again.'

'And let it stay that way,' said Cherry. 'Time to switch off business and on to Toddy's master class in dining.'

We went into small-talk mode and learned more about dining that I ever wanted to know. Everything was excellent, including the right amount of crystallised salt on my steak.

I had reached half way on my wade through the steak. It was Palmer when my phone rang.

'We're at Toddy's having some time out,' I said. 'Want to join us?'

'Not now,' he said. 'Caxton's dead. I'll pick you up in fifteen minutes.'

# CHAPTER ELEVEN

True to his word, Palmer arrived fifteen minutes later and he stared down aghast at our table.

'Are you finished with all this?' he said.

'Yes, I'm ready to go,' I said.

'If you've finished, then you need to put your cutlery at the four o'clock position,' he said. 'How otherwise will the waiter know you've finished? And it's so much neater. I thought you would know better, Shannon. Always had you down as an educated fellow.'

He leaned over and moved my knife and fork till he was satisfied with the angle, and the rest of the table sheepishly, chastened, aligned their cutlery to the proper place. It pays to humour Palmer. You never know when you might need a policeman, even if an anal retentive.

I got up from the table and said I'd catch up with everyone later. I revised that to in the morning, because I could sense a long night ahead.

'What do you know?' I asked Palmer, as we headed down the road.

'Not much, so far,' he said. '999 call to police and ambulance logged at just after nine. Pronounced dead on arrival. Police doctor is waiting for us. He'll tell us more. Large crowd. Nightmare for witness statements — apparently, a barbecue was taking place. We've locked down the crime scene and forensics are on their way.'

'I was invited,' I said. 'Thought our team dinner was more important. I wonder what might have happened if I had been there. Would I have somehow managed to protect her?'

'What can you tell me about the deceased?' he said.

'Nice woman,' I said. 'Looking for the man to love. Used dating sites, if that had any relevance. Chose the wrong man, maybe?'

'Do you really think that?' he said.

'No,' I said. 'Increases the body count at Fairstead. Too big a coincidence. A shame,' I said. 'She was lonely, but good fun, especially compared to what I'd endured from the other consultants at the hospital. We flirted. It was a joke between us. She'd have had shedloads of money from the dividends from the business. I doubt she generated enough revenue to warrant an equal share. Maybe one of the other shareholders decided to cut her out. Money behind it all — first Cooper, now Caxton. A lot of shares to be picked up in advance of the extension.'

We pulled up at a street of terraced houses in the salubrious area of Highgate. The one we sought was spread across three of the houses. Three houses, just one front door. Caxton had knocked three into one. Just what had that cost — purchase prices and conversion — mind-boggling. Talking millions.

Inside, in the garden, there was an eery silence. What had been the hubbub of a party, I guessed, was now filled with low mumblings. The barbecue was still glowing and a small group of guests had huddled around it to catch some warmth as the evening chill set in. I saw the consultants standing there in a group with drinks in their hands — the men adopting an unofficial uniform of black slacks and tweed jackets. Blair — dark blue trouser suit and those red stilettos — was there, too, with an attractive girl in her twenties — white dress, long blonde hair, blue eyes and fresh face making her seem even younger. Innocent. Sweet. There were no WAGs to accompany the men. Would alcohol help or hinder the investigation? If so, who would crack first and slip up to reveal a vital piece of information?

A female police officer came up to Palmer and gave us white coveralls and shoe protectors so we wouldn't contaminate the crime scene. We donned them and followed her inside. Caxton was at the bottom of a flight of stairs looking like a broken doll. Her head was twisted into an impossible position. The police doctor on call was kneeling over her examining the body.

'What have we got?' Palmer said.

'Broken neck,' the doctor said. 'Contusion to the back of the head. Too much alcohol and fell down the stairs, maybe.'

'Or maybe not,' I said.

'Time of death?' the doctor said. 'Obvious. She would have been dead at the time of the 999 request. Hardly a moment prior. It's your call, but I would have thought she'd be missed quickly as she was playing the host and cooking the food. Anyway, I'm finished and off to bed. You can take it from here. Good luck. You'll need it.'

'Before you go,' said Palmer, 'could the fall down the stairs have caused the contusion to the back of the head?'

'Murder? Knock her out first and then push her down the stairs?' the doctor said. 'Eminently possible. Now, time for my hot chocolate, read a few pages of my thriller about a group of mercenaries and drift off to sleep, although somehow I doubt it.'

Two men in white coveralls from forensics stood behind us waiting for the clearance from Palmer to start their work.

'Two theories,' Palmer said. 'Number one. Caxton has too much to drink like the doctor suggested. Easy to do at a barbecue because you can be waiting a long while for food — hard to get your timings right — don't believe in it myself. Not a method I would use — far too messy. Anyway, she comes inside the house to go to the bathroom, falls or trips or something and tumbles down the stairs. Open and shut case.'

'Which we don't buy,' I said. 'The theory we do believe, however, is that she comes in to use the bathroom, but is followed by the murderer who breaks her neck and throws her down the stairs.'

'And what do we have to back up this hunch as to what happened?'

'The group from Fairstead are here. They are all doctors, and would have done all the years of basic training, including anatomy. Who better to know how to break someone's neck?'

We went outside and Palmer found the officer in charge of the SOCO team. He told her to search the grounds as well as the house for a heavy weapon.

It was time to speak to the consultants. Ferguson appeared to be the designated mouthpiece, although I could see Gordon Owen, our cosmetic surgeon, itching to butt in. Unlike him to miss an opportunity to bait me.

'A surprise, Shannon,' Ferguson said. 'I wish I could say "how nice to see you again", but the circumstances preclude that.'

'Can you all tell me what you'd been doing prior to Caxton's death?' Palmer said.

'We were standing together as a group — we really didn't have much in common with the other guests, neighbours mostly, a bit too sure of themselves — advertising executives and estate agents, you know the type. Just sipping a decent red wine and talking about work. It was nice to catch up — there seems to be so little time at the hospital for a proper chin wag of things. I must admit that some of the talk about work focused on Cooper's death. A bit macabre, you might say. Tell us, how did she die? There's a rumour that she fell down the stairs. Is that right?'

'We're keeping an open mind,' Palmer said. 'So did any of you go into the house while you were having your nice little chat?'

'I went earlier to the toilet,' Ferguson said, 'prostate problem. Sorry, too much information.'

'We can never have too much information,' Palmer said. 'Go on.'

'No, I suppose not. Apart from that, we were all here together. I suppose you could say we all alibi each other.'

'Some might say that is convenient,' said Palmer.

'But not you, Chief Inspector, I hope,' said Ferguson.

'No one else with you?' said Palmer. 'Apart from the young lady here?'

'We rather viewed it as business rather than pleasure,' Ferguson said.

'We thought it might be fun,' said Blair, breaking the soliloquy. 'Debbie's always upbeat. Good for a laugh. We thought we might see the current beau, but no such luck, if she had one, that is. She said she was going to barbecue some halloumi for Abby here, who's vegetarian. Seemed like if she was willing to go to all that trouble, then we ought to come along.'

'We'll take formal statements tomorrow at the station — sorry in advance for that,' said Palmer. 'You're free to go. Give your contact details to the officer at the front of the house, and he'll tell you when to go to the station to make your statement.'

As Palmer was about to leave them, Owen stared at me and laughed.

'Pistols at dawn, Shannon?' he said, unable to keep silent any longer.

'I couldn't think of anything better,' I said, as he walked off.

'What's that all about?' said Palmer. 'Alpha male stuff?'

'He had to have the last word,' I said. 'I can't stand him, and he has the same opinion of me.'

'Is that helpful to the case?' said Palmer.

'Who knows?' I said.

'Keep it out of the picture then,' said Palmer. 'Remain impartial. We don't want anything to cloud the issue.'

'Is that what you do?' I said.

'It is,' he said, 'but I always fail. Right, let's go home. Nothing left to do here.'

'One moment,' I said. I picked up a clean glass from the table and poured myself a red wine. Chilean. I sipped. Pretty good. 'I have some news for you. Although I have to temper what I say. I have good news and bad news about Cooper's puzzle. Which would you like first?'

'Oh, let's have the good news. Haven't had much of that recently.'

'We have cracked the code. We think that the common linkage is that the names marked are part of a team used to conduct operations. The ones with question marks are those in another team that he wasn't sure about.'

'And what does that mean?'

'That's the bad news. We don't have a clue.'

'Shannon! Don't do that to me.'

'It's progress,' I said. 'Cooper had sensed something was wrong at the hospital and did some digging. He worked out that it was something to do concerning operations. That's why he was killed. The people involved didn't like him doing that. They had to silence him. We need now to follow his thoughts and find out what he concluded. It's a further step.'

'So are you going to put yourself in the firing line?'

'I thought I might put myself up as bait,' I said. 'Whoever is behind it tried to scare me off. They might be tempted to try another step forward. I was hoping I might get some protection from you.'

'Do you get satisfaction from this?' he said. 'The thrill of the chase, playing the fox role? Are you a danger freak?'

'Must be something in the genes,' I said.

I had another sip — OK, more than just a sip, I confess — of red wine.

'I can't authorise full support. Too many questions would be asked, but I'll have some officers do a round at your home and a drive past the hospital. Ring me anytime and I promise I'll push alarm buttons. We'll be there before you even know it. How many more days will you be there?'

'I should close the contract by end of play Tuesday, but I can stall and spin it out till the end of the week. I can say an urgent call from another client. There's not much they can do about it. They need me to authorise the NHS money for the extension: without that, the plan can't go ahead. Maybe they'll treat me sweeter till I sign the piece of paper.'

'Or maybe they'll just kill you.'

'There is that,' I said. 'A fundamental weakness in the plan, you might say, but if you never take a risk, where is the fun in life?'

'Cherry won't like it,' he said. 'Don't ever let her be alone till the twins are born.'

'I've agreed a deal. To continue I have promised to see a man called Johnny Silver, although for why, I know not.'

'From what little I know of him,' Palmer said, 'you'll be a few rungs up the ladder. Mixing with royalty, almost. He's on our files as a person of interest, but I won't spoil the surprise. Good luck.'

I finished the glass of wine.

'Home, James,' I said.

* * *

Cherry was there in the river room waiting for me. I was touched, but worried.

'What are you doing, darling?' I said. 'You're supposed to be in bed sleeping, not being up waiting for me to return. It's two o'clock in the morning.'

'I couldn't sleep,' she said. 'I've been getting pulses — contractions, maybe. I don't know whether I'm near to birth or not. Plus I was worried for you. There seemed no point in trying to sleep. Forgive me.'

'Nothing to forgive,' I said. 'Sorry if I sounded sharp. Come here.'

She stood up from the Chesterfield and I gave her a great big hug. Well, as close to a great big hug as the bump in her stomach would let me.

'Have you packed a bag?' I said.

'Yes,' she said. 'Arthur carried it downstairs for me. It's in Beryl's office. All ready to go.'

'Bar the shouting,' I said.

'Bar the screaming, more like,' she said. 'Sit with me a moment, and I promise I'll then go bed.'

We sat down and looked at the Thames rolling by. There was no river traffic and the view wasn't interrupted.

'I'm worried,' she said. 'Another death. I sense that things are coming to a head. Promise me you'll take extra care.'

'Promise,' I said. 'There's always Arthur, and Palmer is going to set up more police presence around us all. Soon be over.'

'Thank God.'

'We've found the link behind the ticks on Cooper's list. It's a team around operations. We only have to find out what sort of operations and then the mystery is solved. We need to find out what Cooper discovered. Whatever is behind the murders will be clear. A secret so dark that two people had to die.'

'I forgot to tell that I arranged an appointment with Johnny Silver for Monday at one. I've prepared some background information on him. There's a folder on your desk. I think the two of you will get on. I have a good feeling about it. He may be able to assist you, too. Worth a shot, although don't take that too literally. He's cancelled his flight back to his Caribbean island for this meeting. Make it count for both of you.'

'I trust your judgement,' I said. 'If you say it's good, then I'm looking forward to meeting him.'

'Now tell me about tonight?' she said.

'Debbie Caxton was throwing a barbecue. At some point, she goes inside to use the bathroom. Someone was following her, broke her neck and threw her down the stairs to make it look like an accident. The Fairstead people were there and alibi each other. Dead end. Maybe the forensic people will find out something that will be important.' I paused. 'I'm sad for her. She was unconventional — not like the other consultants with their haughty manner. I liked her attitude, from her denim dungarees to the infectious smile she had when we were flirting. Yes, we flirted, but it was all a game. She was lonely. Apart from that, she had a rich life. Everything you could have wanted. Died too young. I'm going to find the murderer — it's the least I can do.'

'And I believe you will,' she said. 'Let's hope you find him before he finds you.'

# CHAPTER TWELVE

'Take me out,' said Cherry when we finally surfaced on that Saturday morning. 'I want to go somewhere free from all this.' She waved her hand in the air. 'Thrill me!'

It was a bright October morning with a slight breeze blowing from the south. We donned some lightweight jackets and got in the Beamer. I remembered a place I had been from another job that sounded a good fit with her demands. We headed to Southend.

We managed to get a parking spot on the promenade and we could see Adventure Island about half a mile away: about ten minutes, that would be, which would not tax Cherry too much. We walked to the pier, got the train to the end and sat down on a bench looking out over the sea. The tide was out and there were people out for a ramble or walking their dogs. A few intrepid parents and their kids were on the beach making sandcastles. Perfect escape. There was no one trying to kill me.

We went into a small café that had been used for Jamie Oliver's pop-up restaurant and had a watery coffee. Why complain? This was a slice of heaven. A release from the clinical atmosphere of the hospital.

'I'm conflicted,' I said.

'For why?' Cherry said.

'Ferguson,' I said. 'He's supposed to be one of the best gynaecologists in the country, but there might be some risk in going private at the hospital with two people dead. I think we should go NHS, and if we finish up with his registrar doing the C-section, why should we be worried? Probably done lots of caesareans in the past.'

'I was starting to think that way myself,' she said. 'Good to get that decision out of the way. Have you had any thoughts about names?'

'That can wait,' I said. 'We don't even know sex at the moment, and you know how superstitious I am. I don't want to jinx anything. Come on, drink up. Let's go and get fish and chips. You can't come to the seaside without having fish and chips.'

There was a bewildering array of fish and chips restaurants along the sea front. We settled for one where you can sit outside. It was a snap decision and we didn't regret it. Everything tastes better sitting in the open air overlooking the sea.

A thought struck me. I should never have let it cross my mind.

*Is this the calm before the storm?*

* * *

Palmer was waiting for us when we arrived home. 'Don't spoil a perfect day, Dennis,' Cherry said. We were on first name terms now.

'I'm working all weekend. Hard to think that others are not doing the same,' he said. 'Apologies. I won't stay long, just a small update. A cold beer would go down nicely.'

'With a glass and drip mat?' I said.

'Beautiful,' he said. 'I sometimes wonder if you don't know too much about me.'

I refrained from comment, went to the fridge, took two bottles of beer and poured Cherry an orange juice. I flipped the tops off the beer, got two glasses and drip mats and sat down in the river room.

'So what's the latest?' I said. 'What's so urgent that you have to come here on a Saturday?'

'I have fifteen officers working round the clock on this last case, together with the linked murder of Cooper, and we've got nothing. All that stuff you see on the TV about an inspector and sergeant solving murders on their own are poppycock — a word I would substitute with something more vulgar if Cherry wasn't here. We're looking to see whether CCTV cameras on Caxton's house and those of the neighbours have anything helpful. We've taken formal statements from the Fairstead people and have got nothing. They alibi each other and can't remember anything else.'

'Frustrating,' I said. 'It will all change. We're coming to the end game.'

'Nothing like a cold beer to get the creative juices flowing,' he said. 'What's the latest on your side?'

'We took a day off,' I said. 'Valentine and Anji agreed to do the same. They'll be back tomorrow — giving up their Sunday — because they want to know what it's all about. What do we know? Let's recap. Four surviving shareholders, one of which is the killer, no other interested parties. They all have a motive — vaults about to be swollen by bigger profits if the extension goes ahead. Because of something we don't yet know, there is something big going down at the hospital. The attacks on me reek of something bigger than the four of them could have done. I don't see any of them with the knowledge to hire a hit man with a sword. So there has to be someone above them that does the dirty work, and we don't have a clue who it is.'

'The beer's good,' Palmer said. 'About all one can say. I wonder where this will all end.'

'Me, too,' I said. 'Whatever, it will all end soon. With a bit of luck, we'll crack what Cooper found and get a resolution. Any forensics that would help?'

'Checked her phone and nothing useful,' Palmer said. 'Blair had a text with Caxton about mundane things — what to wear, whether she would like a bunch of flowers or bottle of wine? — but nothing else.'

'I suppose we ought to look at the possibility that they're all working in concert — a gang of murderers rather than just one. Cooper finds out what is going on and has to be eliminated. Caxton thinks better of what they have done and becomes a risk, so that she has to die, too. Does that make our task easier or more difficult?'

'More difficult in the sense that they alibi each other,' Palmer said. 'So convenient for them. Easier if one of them cracks and gives evidence against the others.'

'And what are the chances of that?' I said.

'Pretty much zero,' he said. 'Whoever cracks will have a target drawn on their back. Caxton's death shows what happens if you squeal. What are you likely to conclude about recommending the business to the NHS?'

'The business is sound enough,' I said, 'although they take all the profits as dividends rather than keeping something back for investment. That makes them greedy, and greed has no bounds. Financially, I should have to give them a clean bill of health — I've not found any more frauds — but I don't like it. There must be a skeleton in the cupboard somewhere. Do I play it safe and say no, in the light of the murders?'

'Too many dilemmas,' Palmer said. 'Don't envy you.'

'How's your wife?' Cherry said, forcing us to move out of the impossible. It was unproductive.

'Much as usual,' Palmer said. 'Goes on at me if I work too hard and she doesn't see enough of me, or because I don't work enough and I get under her feet.'

'A policeman's lot is not a happy one,' Cherry said. 'Isn't that how the old song goes?'

'And rightly so,' Palmer said. He placed his empty glass on the drip mat and rose to go. 'Look after yourself, Cherry. These are dangerous times, although I've lined up patrol presence around you — here and at the hospital. And as for you, Shannon, don't try going it alone. That's our job, not yours. Look what happened the last time when you went on a vigilante spree.'

'I'd like to say I learned my lesson,' I said.

'But you can't,' he said. 'Sometimes I like to think you can change your habit of a lifetime, and then I see sense.'

* * *

Sunday dawned. Whether it was the sea air or the result of too many broken nights, we slept late. I could hear Anji up and about singing some song I didn't recognise, so was probably current rather than my era. Given a choice, and when alone, I liked to listen to jazz piano from way before my birth. Fats Waller's 'Ain't Misbehaving' seemed to act as a reminder of my life and how at odds with it I was.

I showered, didn't bother with a shave, dressed in denim jeans and a T-shirt and went downstairs. Anji was sitting at my conference table already working.

'Good morning,' I said. 'Can I get you a coffee?'

'That would be good,' she said. 'I lost track of time. Must be almost an hour since my last one.'

I made her a latte and an espresso for myself and carried them into my office. I placed hers by her side and took a seat with mine.

'How are you doing?' I said. 'What are you working on?'

'I'm looking at the sales data, like you suggested,' she said. 'I'm going through all the invoices again and looking at the types of them: hips, cosmetic surgery and so on and then by specific type of operation — boobs, gastric bands, new hips, the list goes on. Trying to make sense of them. It's going to be a long haul, but I have that electric buzz that tells me I'm going to strike it lucky. I heard you come in late on Friday night. Didn't manage to catch you yesterday. What happened?'

'Caxton was murdered,' I said. 'That brings us down to four people who could be the murderer — or murderers, if they are all working in concert.'

'How did she die?'

'Broken neck, made to look like she'd fallen down a flight of stairs.'

'Anything I can do?' she said.

'Thanks for the offer,' I said, 'but it's in Palmer's hands now. I doubt whether he's going to have much luck. Moving on. Let me read out the data and you put it all in a spreadsheet. Might save some time.'

'Fire away,' she said.

We'd worked for an hour when Morag came in.

'Who's for a rib of beef for a traditional Sunday lunch?' she said.

'Yum,' we said.

'That's good,' she said, 'because it's in the oven. One o'clock. Don't be late, or my Yorkshire puddings might deflate and we don't want that.'

'Will there be enough for Valentine, if he comes over?' Anji said.

'Of course,' Morag said. 'I'm catering for Arthur, so I got a triple rib.'

'One o'clock it is, then,' I said.

* * *

'So what do we have to drink today?' I said to Norman, as we sat down at one o'clock on the nose.

'It's a cheeky little Malbec from France,' he said, filling my glass.

'Interesting,' I said, sipping. 'Who would have known it?'

'OK,' he said. 'Someone's got to ask it, so it might as well be me. What are the two of you looking so smug about?'

'We think we've cracked it,' said Anji. 'Well, maybe not exactly cracked it, but putting a critical piece of the jigsaw in the puzzle.'

'Continue,' said Norman, 'before I grow tired of the game.'

'Over to you, Anji,' I said. 'To the victor, the spoils.'

'The biggest income earner is Owen, the cosmetic surgeon,' she said. 'Not only does he do his share of the mundane things — breasts, facelifts, tummy tucks and so on — but he does a lot of facial reconstruction. They can cost the patient as much as fifty thousand pounds. Some of the treatments are paid in cash.'

'Aha,' said Norman, 'you know how much I love cash. Cash is often the key.'

'It does seem to me,' Anji said excitedly, 'or us, I should say, that it does seem a lot of treatments, even though he is supposed to be among the top three in the country. Can there be that many third-degree burns in the country? There is the complication that some of these bills are paid for in a foreign currency, so that does seem that some of the income is from abroad — we need to take that into account. The foreign names reveal that they are related. Seems like a family affair, or multiple treatments for one person. It could all be due to client satisfaction and recommendation.'

Norman carved the beef and put slices on to warmed plates. Morag placed tureens of potatoes and vegetables in the middle of the table. We loaded our plates and poured on gravy and spoonfuls of horseradish sauce.

'Come on, Norman,' I said. 'Ask us for more detail. We're itching to give answers over here.'

'How does this mean we can forge ahead?' he said.

'Great beef, Morag,' Arthur said, losing interest in the conversation.

'What difference does it all make?' continued Norman.

'It looks encouraging,' I said. 'The puzzle is as good as solved. It might give Palmer an opportunity to sweat Owen. Who knows what we might get out of that?'

'From what you've told me,' Norman said, 'he doesn't sound the type of man to confess. He'll bluff it out.'

'Can't do any harm,' I said.

'Apart from saying to the world that you know what they have been getting up to,' said Cherry. 'That makes you a marked man.'

'It could be the opposite,' I said. 'Nothing to hide. I'm not a danger to them anymore.'

'And do you really believe that, Shannon?' said Cherry, reverting to our business mode of names. 'You're putting yourself up as bait. It's a dangerous game you're playing. That's what this all about, isn't it? It's a game, admit it? A game you have to win. I don't like it and neither should you, if you want to stay alive and be a father to our twins.'

'It will soon be over,' I said. 'Everything can then go back to normal. I'm seeing Johnny Silver tomorrow, like you said. I can talk it all through with him as someone independent. No bias.'

'Sorry to interrupt,' said Valentine, 'but how does this affect your recommendation to proceed or not?'

'I've given it a lot of thought,' I said, 'and swung between yes and no, and, taking everything into account, all things being equal and all those other qualifiers, think it has to be a recommendation for the NHS not to go ahead while the murders are unsolved. After that, when we've sorted out all the repercussions, the position may well be different. But overall? Doesn't look like a good bet.'

'Do you still need me tomorrow?' Arthur said.

'No, I'll go straight to the police station and be ready to sit in on an interview with Owen. I'm rather looking forward to it. Then, at one o'clock, I go to Silver's and there won't be anywhere to park. Just respond quickly if I call.'

'That's good,' he said. 'I'm rather hoping for a sandwich of the cold roast beef for my lunch. Unbeatable. Lots of horseradish. Take note, Morag.'

'Someone has to bring us down to earth,' I said, 'and that someone is always you. I can't imagine life without you.'

'Don't get all sentimental on me,' he said. 'I can't cry and eat at the same time.'

# CHAPTER THIRTEEN

Muhammad wouldn't come to the mountain — or should that be the other way round? Whatever, Owen refused to come to the police station and there was nothing that Palmer could do to make him. We sat in the car outside his house. Well, *house* didn't do it justice. It was a mansion with two wings around a massive frontage overlooking the green hills of Hampstead, pretty much one of the most expensive areas of London outside the Monopoly sites of Park Lane and Mayfair.

I expected a butler, but it was Owen himself who opened the door. He smiled at Palmer and scowled at me. He led us through the door and along a central corridor to a room with a large window and French doors to the garden. It was being used as his study and was wide and square, which would have made an impressive dining room, but he probably had one of those elsewhere.

The room contained a campaign desk and matching bookcase with a captain's chair, and four sofas arranged in a square. He gestured us to one of the sofas and sat down on another. He was dressed in an expensive grey three-piece suit with a white shirt and striped tie. His bald head shone in the sun coming through the windows.

'What can I do for you, Inspector?' he said.

'Chief Inspector,' Palmer said.

'Really,' Owen said. 'I would never have guessed it.' *Ouch.* 'And you, Shannon. You seem to pop up everywhere.'

'I'm the bad penny,' I said. 'Always popping up.'

'I regard you more as a mosquito,' he said. 'Buzzing around annoyingly, waiting to bite before it gets swatted. Anyway, enough of chit chat. What can I do for the pair of you?'

Firstly,' said Palmer, 'I'd like to go back to the afternoon of Cooper's death. Remind us of your movements.'

Owen sighed. 'I hope this won't become tedious,' he said. 'As I told Shannon, I was going through a client's notes before an operation. Prep work. Should never be underestimated or omitted.'

'So,' said Palmer, 'no one can vouch for you. No alibi.'

'It's that *alibi* word again,' Owen said. 'Just think how many times in a day when you are on your own, without someone being able to swear to it. That's the way of the world, Chief Inspector.'

'What did you hear when going off to surgery?' Palmer asked.

'Hear? Oh, you mean Cooper playing guitar. Rather better than normal, I thought. Must have practised more than I associated with him.'

If this was supposed to be sweating Owen, it wasn't working.

'Did you have much occasion to use the pharmacy?' I said.

'I was right,' Owen said. 'This is getting tedious. No, I don't have any reason to go in there. That's what the nurses are for. I wouldn't know anything of what drugs are kept where.'

'Let's move on to Caxton,' Palmer said. 'What time did you arrive at the party?'

'Must have been around eight,' he said. 'Can't say precisely, because I didn't look at my watch.'

'Even though it's a Rolex,' I said.

'Ah, is this where it's going? Who has got the better watch? A watch fest, Shannon? I regard the Rolex as an item of jewellery rather than a timekeeping accessory. Before you ask, the others were already there — I like to arrive late and make an entrance. During the whole evening prior to her death, I didn't go inside. Alibi, this time. Compadres.'

'How did you get along with Caxton?' Palmer asked.

'She was a colleague, nothing more. It was rare for me to socialise with her. A trifle shallow, I found. Didn't dress appropriately with her jumpsuits and the like. Needed to be more professional, to be honest.'

'Did you resent the fact that she was getting the same shareholding as you?' I asked.

'We didn't have a feud, if that's what you're asking?' he said. 'I didn't murder her over injustice — if that is what you're implying — or for any other reason. Although I regarded her as very much a junior partner. Her shareholding would be discussed at some stage.'

He took a handkerchief from his pocket and wiped a bead of sweat from his scalp. That was more like it.

'Nice house,' I said.

'Ah, we're getting on to money now, are we, Shannon?' Owen said. 'I confess it's a money pit, but I have more money than I need for upkeep.'

'With the deaths of Cooper and Caxton,' I said, 'your share of the profits goes up from one sixth to a quarter. A substantial increase.'

'Rather fortunate, I admit,' he said, 'but what do the Americans say? That's the way the cookie crumbles.'

'What did you think of Caxton's party?' Palmer said. 'Would you rather not to have been invited?'

'As I told Shannon, if he'd been listening,' Owen said, 'it was all a bit middle class. Dull, would be the best way to sum it up, but I went along with it for the good of the business.'

'Did you talk with her that evening?' I said.

'I look at you two and wonder which is the organ grinder and which the monkey,' Owen said. 'We chatted for a couple of minutes when I first arrived, but she had food to burn, so moved on quickly.'

'What did you talk about?' I said.

'The extension. It has been all about the extension for weeks. You, Shannon, were supposed to bring an end to it. Couldn't have been more wrong.'

'Hard to recommend that the NHS should invest when there's two murders to be solved.'

'How about this, then?' Owen said. 'Caxton murders Cooper, and then commits suicide by throwing herself down the stairs so that she can be the talk of the party? That would be a result for you, Chief Inspector, eh? Case closed, and we could all get back to normal life. Roll the drums.'

I wondered for how long Palmer would let this go on. We were getting nothing but insults from Owen, and I didn't see anything changing. Time to cut our losses.

A phone rang. Owen dug in his pocket and pulled out a mobile. He listened for a moment and said, 'I'm on my way.'

'Saved by the bell,' he said. 'I'm on call and needed urgently back at the NHS hospital. Time to call it a day. I'll show you out.'

He looked at Palmer's car with disgust and was probably hoping none of the neighbours were watching. As we got into Palmer's Sierra — old but immaculate — he climbed into a silver Jaguar and sped off.

'Well,' Palmer said, 'what did we learn from that?'

'Apart from confirming he's an arrogant bastard,' I said, 'nothing.'

'Wouldn't you just love him to be the killer?' Palmer said. 'He wouldn't survive a week in prison with his Rolex and his three-piece suits gone. No one to be impressed. No one to be lorded over. I'd like to be there to watch.'

'From someone who knows,' I said, 'I couldn't agree with you more.'

'Where would you like to be dropped off?' he said.

'Anywhere so I can take a taxi to the City. I've got a banker to see.'

'That's a coincidence,' he said. 'I've got a bank robber to catch.'

'Oh, that life could be that simple,' I said.

'Exactly,' he said.

# CHAPTER FOURTEEN

Silvers was located a stone's throw from the Bank of England down a narrow alley that sums up the ancient City of London and that you could miss quite easily — I did it twice. Any points for perseverance?

I sat in the reception hall of Silvers, banker to the great and good, although where money was concerned, the good was not always what it seemed. From my easy chair in the cavernous ground floor, I had an uninterrupted view of the vast six-storey building with its domed top. Built in the early eighteenth century, it was constructed of stone as solid as the reputation of the bank itself.

I was collected by a slim woman with scraped-back auburn hair in a white blouse, black knee-length skirt and three-inch heels. She was called Bridget, PA to Johnny Silver, non-executive chairman of the bank, and was the epitome of what you would have expected from such an august institution. She looked at me with a puzzled expression on her forehead and led me to the lift, up to the top floor and through the door of Silver's office.

Everything inside was antique and you could almost smell the aromas of a long-gone age of cigars and pipes. His desk was mahogany with a green baize top. The visitor chairs in front of the desk were museum pieces. There was a walnut table and easy chairs in one corner of the massive room. The floor was covered in Persian rugs and the walls had portraits of the Silvers owners going back centuries. I felt I shouldn't touch anything in the room for fear of diminishing its value or offending those who were guardians of the past. And behind the desk sat Johnny Silver. He rose as I entered and approached him.

It was like looking in a mirror. His hair was a little bit shorter than mine and his face was deeply tanned, but the rest was just uncanny. He was the same height, had the same green eyes as me — although there was a glint of steel in them — the same dark hair. He was wearing an obviously hand-made suit in light grey with the faintest of a silver pinstripe. I made a resolution to get one the same. There was a spark of electricity when we shook hands.

'Coffee?' he said.

'That would be good,' I said.

'Espresso?'

'Even better.'

'Double?'

'Perfect.'

'Sugar?'

'Just one,' I said.

He picked up the phone and pressed a key on the handset. Bridget came into the room.

'Two of my usual coffees, please, Bridget,' he said. 'One of the best things I did when coming back here was to buy a decent coffee maker.'

'Good investment,' I said.

'How is Cherry?' he said. 'Must be close to the big day now. We were very impressed with her work.'

'She's fine. Nervous. Doesn't fully know what to expect so she's jittery. Do you have children?'

'Twins,' he said. 'Runs in the family, so I've been told.'

Bridget brought in the coffee.

'See if my mother can come in for tea,' he said. 'Get a Jamaican ginger cake — it's her favourite. She won't pass on learning that.'

'We've each read or viewed a lot about each of us,' I said. 'Time to get the full story.'

'I'll start with what I know about you,' he said. 'I suppose the first time I was aware of you was the death of the Home Secretary. Then the poisoning. Then the drugs bust. As of now, it's the six bullets that have got you into deep water. Everyone says you're a man of honour and I love and respect that. My values. Good work on the youth club, too. You've got a soft streak, Shannon, and a little of that goes a long way. You have the public behind you and that will make sentencing a sensitive issue — we all know that you're guilty — even you have admitted it — so that doesn't really come into it. With your guilty plea, there shouldn't be much of a trial. Your lawyer will use diminished responsibility. That's the only saving grace. I wish you good luck. If you need a good lawyer, I can recommend one.'

'Thanks for the offer, but I have the best. Always good to have the best lawyer.'

'Amen to that,' he said.

We sipped our coffees while wondering who should talk next — was it my turn, or would he continue? I cracked first.

'I don't know why, but I just seem to be a magnet for trouble,' I said. 'Maybe that's just part and parcel of the job — uncovering things that people want buried. Maybe it's something deeper. Part of my DNA? Who knows? The first time I heard anything about you was being rumoured to have played a part in a mass shooting between mafias in Amsterdam. I hope that's true, because that is why I'm here.'

'Like you, I attract trouble,' he said. 'I have a bunch of good friends and we always support each other, look out for each other. Have been willing to die for each other.'

'There's nothing bigger than that,' I said. 'Were the rumours true?'

'Couldn't get much truer,' he said.

'There was a private hospital at the back of it, they say.'

'A lot of bad things were happening there,' he said. 'Someone had to stop it and that someone was us. We had the American mafia on one side and the Russian mafia on the other. Someone — yes, us — just had to set them up against each other. In the end, the good guys and the bad guys both got what they deserved.'

'What was going on at the hospital?' I said.

'In basic terms, they were supplying organ donations to wealthy clients. My wife-to-be was due to be one. We had to act.'

'And then there were subsequent missions,' I said. 'Nothing proved again, but the rumours kept circulating. That's why I need your help. Any of the muttering correct?'

'All of it,' he said with a smile. 'You know, I rather miss those days. I'm here for a couple of days each month casting a watchful eye over things, and the rest of my time running a beach bar in St Jude in the Caribbean. Idyllic life. Be good to have an adrenaline fix from time to time. Going cold turkey is hard.'

'I've got myself in a situation I think I can handle, but I'm worried about what might happen to Cherry and all my friends. If things don't work for me, I'd like you to watch out for them.'

'When is all this going to happen?'

'The next few days,' I said.

'Try to stall it and I'll get as many of my friends as I can out of retirement. Have no fear. Everyone will be well protected.'

'If things get out of control there and illegal actions have to be taken, then I have a problem. My tracker will place me there. I can't be there when things go down or I'm back in prison, post-haste.'

'We'll be back-up,' he said. 'Rest assured.'

'Now we both know the main act is about to come on stage,' I said. 'I'm rather partial to Jamaican ginger cake myself.'

143

'I've got a bottle we can taste in the meantime.'

'Vodka?'

'You got it.'

'Polish?'

'My wife says it's the best.'

'And what man can argue with his wife?'

He took two tumblers from inside a sideboard, added ice from a bucket on the top and poured in a small measure of the Polish vodka. He brought the glasses back to his desk and passed one to me. We sipped and rolled the vodka around our tongues. Smooth and mellow, with a kick as it slid down the throat. He was right; it was the best.

'I've got a friend who can help out,' I said. 'Arthur. Cell mate from Brixton. Ex-professional wrestler. Unfazed by most things. I'd trust him with my life — have done in the past and he's never let me down. Be a good man to have on your side in a spot of trouble.'

'Always good to have another man on your side,' Silver said. 'Does he shoot?'

'God, no,' I said. 'Strictly heavy. Can handle himself in a fist fight or against a knife.'

'He'll do fine,' Silver said. 'Now, why don't I take you on a tour of the building while we wait for the Empress of Silvers?'

He rose from the desk and we walked out of the office. We spent a moment looking down at the floors below. 'Impressive, huh?' he said.

'Definitely,' I said. 'How many people work here?'

'Around five hundred at any given time. Some do a lot of travelling because of our international business — offices in the States and in Amsterdam, too, but clients all over the globe.'

We walked around each level, poking our noses through the doors of individual offices. While the exteriors around the stairwell retained the look of the bygone era, the insides were up to date, with screens sitting on top of craftsman-made desks and water coolers on each floor. There was a restaurant on the top floor big enough to cater for everyone with two sittings. And surrounding everything was the solidity of stone. This was a good place to work, shielded from the hustle and bustle in the streets of the city. Tranquil. Smiley faces all around.

'We operate a profit-sharing scheme for staff,' Silver said. 'We pay our people well and only take the best. You couldn't find a better place to work anywhere in London.'

'I might question that,' I said.

'OK. Excluding yours,' he said.

Tour over, we took the lift back to the top floor and into his office. The small circular table was laid with a tea tray with three cups and saucers, milk, sugar and an aromatic ginger cake with small plates, napkins and forks. We took seats at the table and waited for the guest of honour.

At three o'clock precisely, Bridget knocked and entered. Beside her was a short woman of indeterminate age, but who must have been at least seventy years old. She had silver hair — appropriately — cut in a way so that it framed her face. She had the green eyes I expected from seeing Johnny. It was an unmissable trademark of the Silver dynasty. She stared at me.

'This is Mother,' said Johnny. 'No better introduction. I'll pour.'

'Welcome,' Mother said. 'Welcome to the Silver family. You know, Johnny, I'll take a splash of brandy in mine.'

'How much is a splash?' he said.

'A lot,' she replied 'Pleased to meet you, Mr Shannon. I will be formal for a while, if you don't mind.'

Johnny went to the sideboard, opened a cupboard door and picked out a bottle of fine XO Bisquit brandy. The best you can get. Too good for adding to tea in normal times, but this was to be a special occasion. He poured a very decent amount of cognac into Mother's cup and poured a straight tea into his and mine.

'In case you think I'm a lush,' Johnny said, 'the brandy is only for medicinal times.'

'I might develop some minor ailment,' I said, 'but I've had the vodka and that must be my limit till I get back.'

There was some tea drinking to be done before the denouement and we were silent for a while.

'Time for some answers, Mother,' Johnny said. 'I think you've been holding out on us. Take it from the top. I suspect it all began with a birth — no, make that two births.'

'You know that you were illegitimate, Johnny. I revealed that a while ago after you saved your half-brother Carlo. The name of your biological father was kept secret until then and remains secret to the outside world. Just you and me know the answer. But that wasn't the end of the secret. Your supposed father knew you were illegitimate, and we argued about it. He wanted to give you away. I couldn't have that.'

She took a large bite of her slice of ginger cake as if in need for sustenance.

'But the worst was yet to come. When I gave birth, it was twins. A touch more brandy, Johnny, if I may.'

She helped herself to another slice of cake.

'Excellent,' she said.

'Stop stalling, Mother,' said Johnny. 'The cake will still be there when you finish the story.'

'Your biological father is your Uncle Gus,' she said.

'You must meet Gus,' Johnny said. 'He is the kindest, most gentle man you could meet, and full of wisdom.'

'Your legal father never learned about Gus. It was a secret I never revealed to him — God rest his soul. He was furious that it was twins. He demanded that both boys be given away. We argued incessantly. In the end, we reached a compromise. One boy, Johnny, would be raised by us and the other would be fostered. All we knew of the foster parents was that they came from Ireland. By the physical likeness of the two of you, I think that you, Nick, must be that fostered boy. Story over. We can have DNA tests, but I think the link is evident. Welcome to the family, Nick.'

She got up from her chair, shook the crumbs off her dress, and came round to stand over me. 'Give me a hug, son.'

I did as she said, and there was a spark of electricity between us — static from the rugs, or something more fundamental than that?

'I've thought about it, Johnny,' I said. 'I'll have that other vodka after all.'

While he poured, I thought about how my life had been turned upside down. The girl I thought of as my sister — the girl whom I helped to commit suicide, the girl for whom I had spent seven years in prison — was no blood relation after all. Would I have acted any differently if I had known that? No. It was something inside me. Something elemental. Indescribable. I took a large sip of the vodka while I tried to process everything.

'Where do we go from here?' I asked.

'Let's divide it up into short term and long term,' Johnny said. 'Short term is the problem you have in the hospital.'

'Two murders now,' I said, 'and I suspect I might be the third. It could be necessary to put some sort of raid on the hospital. I'll draw you a plan of the layout and where you can find everything.'

'I'll contact my friends, get them over here to meet you,' Johnny said. 'One of the team is the planner — Stan the plan, you might call him. He'll work through all the options with you.'

'I'm worried about Cherry,' I said. 'Two unsolved murders. Whoever is behind them doesn't have any limits. Her gynaecologist works privately at the hospital. We can't take the risk of him holding Cherry as a hostage, if he's involved. We've cancelled our plan of using him to do a C-section and will use the NHS hospital instead. With luck I can resolve the case before she might deliver, but we have to plan for anything that might happen. When can you be on standby?'

'Two days at the earliest; three more likely,' he said. 'My friends are all in different countries, so travel arrangements might be critical. I'll start calls to them later today.'

'Are you sure about this, Johnny?' Mother said. 'You've been out of action for a while. Can you still handle it?'

'I'm bored, Mother,' he said. 'I need action. I suspect others may feel this way, too. Just one more mission to get the adrenaline pumping through our brains. Hell! Let's go for it.'

'And you, Nick?' she said. 'Do you really have to do this? Why not walk away?'

'Because I signed a contract,' I said. 'To renege on that would have no honour. Promises must be kept.'

She sighed. 'I've only just met my other son. Don't let both of you be snatched away from me now.'

'You can trust us,' I said. 'Good teams can't be defeated.'

'Amen,' she said.

'That's it, Ma,' we said simultaneously.

# CHAPTER FIFTEEN

'Do you believe in fate?' I said to Cherry as she rested in the leather rocking chair on our floor of the building. I could tell she was in discomfort as she wiggled around continuously trying to find the best position for her body with the twins inside.

'You mean in general, or Johnny Silver in particular?' she said.

'Both, I suppose. That whatever course I might have taken in my life, this moment was predestined. We were only ever going to meet up along the way.'

'Wow,' she said. 'It's a big concept for a pregnant woman to philosophise on when getting close to delivery and her mind is permanently fixated on future outcomes, but I think the same view might be taken of us getting together. Who would ever have thought it?'

'It's like whatever one does, the future has been written,' I said. 'You could also say the same about Buzz. One crossed path led to youth clubs rather than living on the street with a knife in his pocket.'

'It's not a comforting thought,' Cherry said. 'Powerlessness is the word that comes to mind. Do you mean that whatever we do, the twins will be born at the appointed time at the appointed place? That the future has already been written in the stars?'

'Something like that,' I said. 'I believe Johnny Silver has a part to play in our history. It isn't all about the past; it's the future, too. When did you think that something odd was about to take place?'

'From the very first time I met him. The likeness — both physical and mental, your outlook on life and moral code — was too much to be random. I feel relief that he is involved in our future. I know we're a good team here, but his involvement is reassuring — we are not alone.'

'What do you think of his eyes?' I said. 'That's the only difference between us. There's a coldness about them. I suppose it's nurture rather than nature, given his history as a mercenary, but I felt I had to look away. He radiates steel. It says, "Don't cross me or I will take your life away. I will not think twice. Oppose me and you will lose everything."'

'Did he tell you about his wife, Anna?' Cherry said. 'It would fit into your view that the future is marked out and whatever you do, you will end up in the same position. He and Anna were unlikely souls that shared a common feature — intense love. Get him talking about her when the vodka is flowing. Fascinating story.'

The mention of vodka sounded a different note. I got up from the sofa and went to the drinks hidden inside the oversized globe. Made me think about how small we were in the great scheme of things. I poured a measure over ice and asked Cherry if there was anything I could get her. She smiled and shook her head. She did more wriggling and I sat down with my vodka. 'Anything new?' I said.

'Getting close now,' she said. 'Won't be long. It's like two children inside me training for the Olympics. They never keep still. I'm hoping it's a sprint rather than a marathon.'

'I've been googling C-sections and it seems they can do it with local anaesthetic rather than general. Neither of us will miss a moment of the miracle that is birth.'

'I must admit,' she said, 'that I don't find that comforting. Being awake while they slice me up with a scalpel. Urggh! Let's change the subject. You're going to advise the local NHS hospital not to go ahead with the part-funding of the extension, aren't you? Doesn't that worry you? Up till now the focus has been taking you away from the decision and influencing the result. What if they switch to revenge?'

'I can't influence that,' I said. 'My time has to be focused on the probable rather than the possible. I'll always try to have a Plan B, though.'

'And a C as well?' she said.

'And a C as well,' I said.

'You know what I'm going to say?'

'That we can't keep living this way,' I said. 'On the edge of the precipice all the time, waiting for the scale to slip the balance over the edge. A fine line to live with. But if my future is predetermined, why should I change? Pointless.'

'That might be how it's construed,' she said. 'Then my plea for a safer life would be pointless, too? It seems you win whatever I do. That I should roll over and admit defeat. Hardly seems fair. I know what you're thinking — whoever said life was fair? And whoever said it has my undying anger.'

The philosophical debate was interrupted by the sounds of screaming down below. I raced downstairs to find that the screams were coming from outside. Norman, a wily old bird, had fitted bars to the downstairs windows, plus bullet-proof glass and an exterior fitting of metal gauze designed to make anything thrown against them to bounce off them, as well as the penetration of mosquitoes, with which we didn't have a problem. Good move, though.

I opened the door to find a Molotov cocktail sending fierce flames into the air. The weapon had bounced off the gauze back to its attacker. A man stood there with flames consuming his body, vainly trying to put them out by frantic patting of his hands. The screams of pain filled me to the bone. I rushed back inside and found the fire extinguisher in Morag's room and then back outside with my hand on the control lever. I started spraying. It made little difference to the burning man. I used the whole extinguisher before he hit the ground. I dialled Palmer, much to his wife's consternation, I expected. I thought about telling her about waste disposal units. Rest assured, I phoned for an ambulance, too. It had all the hallmarks of an injury for which Owen's skill would be needed. If the attacker lived, that is. I didn't fancy the odds for that.

I walked back inside and found a buff envelope on the mat. It contained two sheets of paper. One said simply, 'Sign this'. The other was a letter to the head of the NHS hospital saying that I recommended their investment in the new extension at Fairstead. Fat chance! *Que sera, sera.*

* * *

Palmer was thrilled to see me. 'Not you again, Shannon,' he said. 'You're a one-man crimewave. I'm thinking of just moving in here to cut down my carbon footprint.'

'If you did that, who would catch your bank robber?'

'I suspect he's disappeared already,' he said morosely. 'Back to his villa on the Costa del Crime until he fancies another dip into a bank's purse. The ambulance team don't expect your attacker to live. Even if he did, I doubt whether he would talk. There's some nasty people out there, all of them focused on taking you out of the picture. How much longer is this going to go on?'

'Just another few days,' I said. 'I have one more thing to set up and then I will deliver the final report — it won't be favourable. Then that should be the end of it.'

'Bar revenge,' Palmer said.

'Funny you should say that,' I said. 'Cherry just used the same word.'

'You should listen to her more often,' he said, 'but I don't know whether you listen to anyone. You seem to have a charmed life, Shannon. One day your luck will run out.'

'But not today,' I said.

'One more thing to set up?' he said. 'Do I want to know what that is?'

'Better not,' I said. 'I'm not sure if I even know what it is yet.'

'But is it legal?' he said.

'Not exactly,' I said.

'Is your definition of legal the same as mine?' he said.

'I suspect not,' I said.

'So, we have "not exactly" and "suspect not". Doesn't make me feel comfortable inside. Best not to book any leave, then?'

'That would be wise,' I said. 'Change of subject. Getting anywhere with the Caxton murder?'

'What do you think? he said. 'No convenient diary with all her inner thoughts nicely laid out for a hard-working policeman to make critical leads. Our officers didn't find anything on her computer that would be useful. Phone, I've already reported to you. Nothing suspicious there. Another dead end.'

'Any good me looking at anything?'

'We may be slow,' he said, 'but we're thorough. I don't think you'll be able to milk something out where we have failed. Thanks for the offer, though. I'll take a raincheck.'

'Carry an umbrella, too,' I said. 'Cover all the angles. Let that be our mantra.'

# CHAPTER SIXTEEN

It was Tuesday morning and Blair was still in combative mood. I was not forgiven for whatever it was I had done to offend her, although I suspect that it was just me being me. I sat down opposite her in her office because I wasn't sure she would offer me a seat. The situation would only get worse. I slid a sheet of paper across the desk.

'I'm doing this out of courtesy,' I said. 'These are the conclusions that will form the critical part of the final report.'

'Pretty bleak,' she said. 'You don't take prisoners, do you?'

'There are several things that worry me. Two murders here with no progress on finding out the culprits. A new CEO to recruit and fit into the role here.'

'I told you,' she said. 'I have found someone with the pedigree to replace Cooper. She can start almost immediately. I gave you her CV. What if I get her in to meet you?'

'Can't do any harm,' I said, 'but there is another matter. The money that you take in dividends. It makes it seem that you don't have faith in the business. That you're not willing to invest any of your own money. Not a good tone.'

'I would have to talk to the other shareholders for that. Too big a step for one person to make. What if I can get some agreement on that?'

'Again,' I said, 'it can't do any harm. I would suggest that the shareholders agree to not take any dividends for two years and invest that money towards the cost of the extension.'

'Give me some time, Shannon,' she said. 'Give me to the end of the week before submitting your report. I'll arrange for the new CEO to come in and I'll talk to the others about the dividends. Surely, a few days won't make any difference. Give me an invoice, including working to close of play on Friday, and I'll pay the money today. I can't say fairer than that. Give me a chance, Shannon.'

She hit my soft spot, I can't stand seeing a woman beg.

'Close of play on Friday then.'

'You won't regret it.'

Oh, how I wish that.

\* \* \*

Blair did not waste any time. She knocked politely on my door and poked her nose through. That's better. She was still wearing those red shoes with the killer heels, this time themed with a skirt suit two inches below the knees. I wondered if she did not find it boring wearing the same shoes every day. Was the statement they made — *you can't judge me* — too much to lose?

She said the CEO designate would be coming in to see me at three o'clock and it would be fitting if I used Cooper's old office for the interview. I told her it was no problem, which was good because I was basically filling in time. I'd gone through the accounts so many times I was becoming number blind. Blair passed the CV to me for a second time in order to prepare my questions. I had asked Morag for the invoice up to Friday and to send it by email. I told Blair she should look out for it.

The CEO designate was called Helen Jacobs and Christine showed her into Cooper's old office at the strike of three. Punctuality is always a good start.

She was average height but seemed shorter because she was severely overweight. A tad going to obese, if not already

155

there, depending on your point of view. I wondered if someone there who was wanting a tummy tuck would have confidence to be involved with someone who needed one. She was wearing a loose-fitting blue trouser suit with a light blue blouse with 'sensible' shoes. The clothes had an aroma hanging on them, telling me she had just had a cigarette. She should fit in well with Blair's secret habit. Her hair was cut just above shoulder length and framed her face. It moved whenever she turned her head, meaning she was constantly sweeping it out of her eyes. It would have annoyed me no end, but then maybe I was just too pragmatic.

Her CV told me she was forty, in a relationship, with two daughters who were currently at different good universities. Helen had graduated with an upper second at Bristol and then did a master's in accountancy. Her job history could have told two stories — either she was practised at a range of skills and, therefore, sufficiently experienced to cope with her new role or, perhaps, she was prone to itchy feet. CVs tell you a lot but very little of importance. Who was she? What motivated her? Would she have people skills?

'You seemed to have moved around a lot,' I said. 'Four jobs in the last ten years. Tell me why that is?'

'Always wanting to stretch myself,' she said. 'Whenever I feel a need for a new challenge, I have to take it on. Onwards and upwards, I suppose.'

Low marks on loyalty, then.

Time to throw in some curveballs.

'Are you a dog person or a cat person?' I said.

'Is this relevant?' she said.

'Dogs have owners; cats have servants,' I said.

'I don't have pets,' she said.

'So, you don't have to take dogs for a walk at six o'clock in the morning, or deal with cats bringing in half-dead wild kill through the cat flap.'

'I suppose so,' she said.

She had used *suppose* twice already and we'd only just begun. Unsure of herself? Too ready to agree?

'What do you do when you get back home after a hard day in the office?' I said.

'It depends on whether my partner is working that day — she's an actor and so can be "resting" at times. I like to cook, so if she isn't at home, I will prepare a meal for her return.'

'What do you cook?' I said.

'Something homely — we always have a full Sunday roast with all the trimmings. During the week, maybe casseroles, toad in the hole. Comfort food. I really can't see where all this is leading,' she said. 'I thought you would be asking technical questions.'

'For which you would have fully prepared,' I said. 'You would be driving the interview and only telling me what you wanted. Do you trust me, Helen? Do we go on?'

'Of course,' she said. 'I suppose so. Do carry on.'

'What sort of car do you drive?'

'I have a Volvo,' she said, 'probably too big for us now the children have moved on.'

Volvo — safe, solid, reassuring, lasts for years. Interesting. Supportive of her partner. Would be good to know her screen name to see if I had come across her in some roles played and whether I recognised her face. Was she a contributor to the household budget or might she be a sponger? Sitting at home all the time watching daytime TV?

'Where would you like to go on holiday, if I was picking up the tab?'

'Gosh. I don't know,' she said. 'Somewhere exotic, I think. The Caribbean, maybe. Somewhere inclusive where you could be waited on hand and foot and lie in the sun.'

Not very imaginative. Basically, get rid of those daily chores and for someone else to meet every whim of her actor partner.

'What do you like to drink after a stressed day?'

'A large gin and tonic with ice and a slice of lemon.'

'Any particular gin?' I said.

'Just as long as it's alcoholic, any brand.'

Not a discerning drinker, but she was welcome to indulge a large glass to soothe away the stress of a hard day. I couldn't criticise. Goodness me, no.

'How long have you known Susan Blair?' I said. The meat of the interview was coming.

'On and off, a few years maybe. We go to the same restaurants and bars. It's very casual. I'm sure our friendship didn't affect Susan's job offer. Not nepotism. Nothing like that.'

'How do you feel about filling dead man's shoes?' I said.

'It's a role I feel confident about,' she said. 'I have the experience and expertise to fill that role. It's like destiny.'

'I was thinking more about the current situation involving his death and the fact that a murderer is still at large?'

'Susan said that there was no danger in the job. There was no reason why I would be at risk.'

'And you believe her?'

'No reason not to,' she said.

'Even though there was a second murder — Debbie Caxton.'

'Susan said Debbie fell down some stairs. An unfortunate accident.'

'For Cooper to be murdered, there would have to be something he discovered,' I said. 'What if you discovered it, too?'

'But you would have gone through the accounts. Given them your approval. What could there be?'

'That's what we all want to know.'

'I'm sure you will find that Caxton's death is just a coincidence. I have no worries about being vulnerable.'

What had Susan Blair said that made this woman feel no fear? She must have dressed the job up with silver paper and a big gold bow. How can a person feel confident of their safety when you might be sitting next to a murderer?

'What did Susan say about shareholding?' I said.

'That if things went well, I could be allowed some shares, maybe after a probationary period. I think everything will be perfect. I can't wait to get stuck into the job.'

'You are more experienced than I at interviews. What is the question I should have asked?'

There was silence from her. Do you bluff it out with an unwelcome truth or keep quiet?

'Nothing that would embarrass me, I think.'

'Thanks for coming in,' I said. 'I'll talk to Susan and we can go through the necessities. I should have said how you will be able to leave without three-months' notice before you would be released?'

'A good relationship, I suppose.'

*Suppose* again.

We shook hands and I showed my caring personality by taking her back to reception. Or maybe I was already guilty of being first to judge?

What did I learn? She was solid — a safe pair of hands. Reliable. Everything so ordinary. She could do the mechanics of the job easily given her job record, I had no doubt, but lacked imagination. I doubted she would ever reach the conclusions Cooper's investigation revealed of whatever got him killed. Overall verdict — she was dull. No threat to the status quo. Itchy feet would worry me, but plenty of time to sort that out. Nothing to object to. Damned by faint praise.

\* \* \*

On my return, everyone was in the river room waiting for the sun to get over the yardarm. I felt like being rebellious, so poured myself a vodka and orange juice anyway.

'What would cause you to keep changing jobs?' I said to the assembled crew.

'Boredom,' said Anji.

'Money, maybe,' said Valentine.

'Stuck in a rut,' said Cherry. 'Not being recognised for what you put in. Going nowhere. Glass ceiling, perhaps?'

'Does that signal a lack of initiative?' I said. 'Maybe a succession of bad choices? Not being able to pick out the good prospects from the bad? As much your fault as your employer's.'

'You know what I think,' Norman said. 'I vote with Valentine. It's all about the money.'

'You're maybe right. I have this woman who is in a relationship with a female actor who spends a lot of time resting, as they say. My candidate for the job, because of this, may well need as much money as possible to substitute for what her partner doesn't contribute to the household expenses.'

'What else bugs you?' said Cherry.

'What if the short-termism suits the employer?' I said. 'The ability to cut an employment before the candidate gets pushy or, in our circumstance, knows too much?'

'Aren't we going around in circles here?' Valentine said. 'Whichever path we follow leads us back to the murders?'

'About which,' said Anji, 'we don't have a clue. Going round in circles and always finishing in a dead end. You would think that a combination of police and Palmer on one side and us here would have been enough to crack the puzzle. Changing tack — and I know it's not our business or remit — I think the hospital should offer a discounted family scheme. Some of the ones with foreign names come back repeatedly for a range of treatments. Just a thought.'

'And a good one, too,' I said. 'Anything to provide some blue sky among the nimbostratus clouds of the final report. Heavy, threatening to rain or snow.'

'So, new contract on Monday?' Morag said.

'What work comes next?' I said.

'I've got some missing funds — probably embezzling — for you and Anji,' Morag said, 'and a valuation of shares prior to a merger for Valentine and Cherry. I thought if you did the interviews, then Cherry can work from here, maybe with Norman's help.'

'Does that work with you?' I said to Cherry.

'I'd just get bored with nothing to do,' she said. 'I don't know how long before birth I have to go, but you'd better get the most out of me while you can.'

'Let's trade projects,' I said. 'I'll lead on the share valuation and Cherry does the embezzlement with Norman's help — you can't have anyone more qualified on that than Norman.'

'I'll do a new plan,' said Morag.

'I'd like to let Anji's wings fly. I'll pass over some of the interviews this time. Brace yourself, everyone, things are likely to get busy.'

And weren't they.

# CHAPTER SEVENTEEN

I had a call from Johnny Silver saying his crew would all be with him in the afternoon and we fixed a time to meet — one where we wouldn't feel guilty to have a beer to seal the deal. He said to bring Arthur. Everything was moving on apace. Soon we would finish the Fairstead hospital job, and then there would be no reason why we would need to be threatened.

Palmer dropped in at midday and Beryl conjured up some ham and mustard sandwiches cut into precise triangles and accompanied by small plates with napkins and drip mats. There were two cold beers in frosted glasses purely to make use of the drip mats.

'How's the hunt for the bank robber going?' I said.

'We had word from a reliable snout that the bank robber was in town for a job. We've searched high and low and can't find hide nor hair of him, if you don't mind mixed metaphors. Oh for the times when they all wore striped jumpers and carried bags marked SWAG over their shoulders. What's going down at Fairstead?'

'I'm no one's best friend,' I said. 'I'm about to call a halt on any funding from the NHS for the new extension. I've agreed to delay my report till close of play on Friday, but it won't make any difference. The new CEO is as dull as ditchwater — I can use metaphors, too.'

'Isn't that a simile?' he said.

'What's a simile between friends?' I said. 'Any progress on our murders?'

'Dead ends,' he said.

'Same here,' I said.

'I'm starting to release officers for other duties. Can't justify so big a team anymore. If you can't find a murderer within the first week, then the chances of solving the crime become very low. It won't be long till it turns into a cold case with minimum crew. Shrug your shoulders and get on with life.'

'Doesn't sound like a good system,' I said.

'But it's the one we've got,' Palmer said.

'Do you understand now what I did with those bullets?' I said. 'You shouldn't have to take the law in your own hands to get justice.'

'I would suspect that the balance of the population would agree with you, but there has to be rules, otherwise the world becomes anarchy. It may have its faults, but it's the best we've got. Sometimes you just have to go with the flow and make the best of it.'

'Acceptance,' I said. 'Not something I'm good at.'

'You were born in the wrong time, Shannon,' he said. 'You should have been one of the knights of the round table in a futile quest to find the holy grail. Heroic, but unsuccessful. Always left unfulfilled. I admire you, but feel for your inevitable loss. You're a good man, Shannon.'

'All it takes for evil to triumph is one good man to turn his back,' I said.

'I'll drink to that,' Palmer said.

\* \* \*

Arthur and I were escorted straight to the boardroom. It was a room of majestic proportions with an oak table seating around sixteen people. There was a matching oak sideboard where a range of hot and cold drinks were set out on the top together with a plate of chocolate digestives. We were humbled. By the room, not by the biscuits, although that was a nice touch.

The door opened and Johnny Silver stepped into the room followed by four men, each singular in their way.

Silver did the introductions. There was a giant of a man, black as ebony and the same height as Arthur — six foot five. He had a shaven head and was called Bull and was Jamaican. And he was frightening.

The next was a six-foot man with blond hair and a handsome face. He was called Pieter and came from South Africa. He, we were told, could charm the pants off a woman at twenty paces. Then there was Stan — Stan the plan, as he was called by Silver — Polish, tall and with a sombre expression. The next was a tall man called Red. He had dark hair and the skin colour of a half-blood Native American. We shook hands, Bull and Arthur sizing each other up. They made a formidable pair.

There was something that bound them all together — those eyes of steel. The look of someone who would kill an opponent at the slightest provocation. Evil would not be tolerated by these men. I was glad they were all on my side.

We helped ourselves to drinks and sat down at the table. Johnny waved a hand at me to tell my story.

'From what you might have known of me from Johnny — my dear brother, we have learned — here's a bit more detail. I have a problem. I am working on a case which has involved the murder of two people, neither of which have the police solved. Someone has been trying to frighten me off. There has also been an attack on my offices and home. Molotov cocktail. Could have been bad, but luck was on my side. The case is about a private hospital that is looking for funding for a new extension. I don't want to give up — it's not in my nature, which I'm sure you now understand — so I need protection for my family, including a heavily pregnant wife fit to burst any day now, and friends at home, and then for me while I'm finishing off the job at the hospital. The police are giving my home some drive-throughs, but that didn't accomplish anything to prevent the last attack. I'm glad to welcome you all to London and answering the call to arms from Johnny. I'm reassured by your presence.'

'We normally operate with weapons,' said Stan. 'What do we need for this job? I have contacts who could provide some Kalashnikovs.'

I winced.

'Guns are out of the question,' I said. 'I have a good relationship with the police, but they would come after us like a ton of bricks if any guns are involved. Nothing I would be able to do. No, it's a case of presence as a deterrent rather than an attack.'

'Sitting in front of you,' said Bull, 'are the five best shoot-ers in the world, and you want us to give up that advantage?'

'I'm afraid so. From what I know about you, I'm sure Stan could work up a plan.'

'Tell me more,' said Stan.

'My home and offices are together in Docklands — easy for travel by train. Parking for a couple of cars if we need to hire some. The hospital is about five miles away, plenty of parking. I only need help for a couple of days while I finish off the job. Afterwards, we have dinner at one of the best restaurants in the world and say our farewells. Couldn't be more simple.'

There was an electric atmosphere in the room — no guns was a problem, it seemed.

'I've finished up much of the work at the hospital,' I said. 'Just in case you need to protect me there, I've drawn a rough plan.'

I took out a sheet of A3 paper and placed it on the table. No one looked at it apart from Stan. It was his job to plan. They trusted him with their lives.

'One person on reception?' he asked.

I nodded.

'Consulting rooms and patients on the ground floor,' Stan said. 'Two operating theatres at one end. Second floor just offices or overspill rooms for patients. Any alarm system we need to know about?'

'Not that I'm aware of,' I said. 'There's probably some form of alarm for out-of-office hours, but I don't feel that that should be a problem. They're open all the time to monitor patients throughout the night. Plus the fact I don't think I need to see anybody outside office hours.'

'Just two points of entry?' Stan said. 'One being the main entrance. The other leading off the kitchen to the bin area?'

I nodded.

I was getting used to this form of clipped dialogue. There were times words were not needed.

'Why are you doing this?' I asked.

'Because Johnny said "pretty please",' Bull said. 'Plus the fact that we miss the action. One more job would give us the excitement we prize. Hard to go cold turkey. Just one more fix.'

'There is the problem that I'm out on bail and wearing a tracker. If anything goes down at the hospital, the police would know I was there. It would show my presence.'

'What about you, Arthur?' said Bull.

'Ex professional wrestler,' he said. 'I can handle myself against anything bar a gun — which seems to be the order of the day. I want to be part of the team.'

'We could do some arm wrestling when the action is slack,' said Bull, with a smile.

'Sounds like a plan,' Arthur said.

'The plan,' said Stan. 'We divide into three units. One protects your home and office; one shields Nick here. The third will be on standby to cope with any changing situation and as relief for units one and two. We will need three cars, each capable of holding all of us. Johnny has booked us a hotel, and we will provide protection round the clock. Anyone who hasn't brought dark clothing needs to buy some. Any questions at this stage?'

Everyone nodded.

'Your media profile is pretty much viral,' Pieter said. I loved his refined accent, as if he had gone to an English public school. I later learned that South Africans often had elocution lessons. 'How much is that likely to affect us?'

'I'm headline news everywhere,' I said. 'The paparazzi would kill for a photo, the tabloids for a front-page story. I'll stay in the background and will liaise through Johnny and Arthur. It has to be low profile for me, but I will try to pull my weight if needed. Everything I know about self-defence, I have learned from Arthur. I won't be a hindrance, if it comes to a fight.'

'When do we start?' Stan said.

'You already have,' I said.

'I like your style,' said Pieter. 'You should fit in well. I think it's time for handshakes to seal the deal.'

And that's what we did.

# CHAPTER EIGHTEEN

The next morning I had a call from Buzz, who had been a natural choice for being in charge of the youth project in a couple of rundown sites in east London: on our side, Valentine was the link person, with Norman doing a wonderful job on the figures for the charity we had set up. Buzz was just fourteen years old and as streetwise as they come. His intervention in my shooting of the assassin had gone viral and the public, without asking, had raised millions of pounds for this club and similar schemes across the country. Buzz was a hero of the nation's hearts.

I took Anji and Valentine along, as it seemed a long time since they'd had fresh air and we were effectively stalled until the Fairstead job was out of the way. It would make a good break for all of us.

Buzz's youth project was situated in what was a former hairdressers and a second-hand furniture store: the wall between the premises had been knocked down and reinforced and now made a double-fronted building for the area's teens. Buzz had matured massively since being in charge and he was justifiably proud of everything that had been achieved. He hugged me. There was a magnetic bond between us. Stop it or I'll cry.

The walls were painted a light green and, in spite of my first thoughts, actually worked. It was cool, calming and inviting. This was a place for everyone.

To provide protection, Red and Arthur followed behind us — Pieter took over Red's duty at the wharf. Red, driving, stuck to us like glue: no, make that superglue. He was the fastest driver I had experienced, and frightening. I'd not seen Arthur tremble for a long while.

On entry to the premises on the left-hand side, which had previously been dominated by the sinks for hair washing, there were two youths playing pool and, behind them, four playing a doubles table tennis game. Four others were watching them sat on white plastic chairs, awaiting their turn, I guessed. We walked through to the back into what had been converted into a kitchen area with a fridge, oven, hob and microwave.

'What can I get you?' Buzz asked. 'Hot or cold, we can give you anything you want.'

'Coffee,' I said. 'As black as it comes.'

'The same for us,' Valentine said.

Anji's entry had not gone unnoticed and boys kept finding excuses to poke their heads inside to see if she was as beautiful as described by the others when she had first walked in.

Buzz made us coffee — instant, but not the cheapest brand — and he led us through to the other side of the premises. There was a big screen TV, another pool table and lots of chairs. We sat down and sipped our coffee.

'How is school going?' I asked. 'Are you sticking to attendance rather than just lounging around?'

'Yes,' Buzz said. 'It's not the best activity going down, but everybody knows it is a deal that we have to adhere to. We made a bargain with you, Mr Shannon,' he said, 'and, following your code, we must fulfil it. Isn't that right?'

I nodded. I would have to follow my head side, as the heart would choke me up.

'The Sharks fitting in?' I asked. The Sharks had once been the sworn enemies of Buzz's gang.

'One big happy family,' Buzz said.

'Finances?' I said.

'Lots of local sponsors,' Buzz said. 'Everyone wants to support the project. Your Mr Gerald came down to see us. He gave us the TV and dish.'

Mr Gerald was in fact Sir Gerald Campion, chairman of Zeus, but I guessed he cut them some slack.

'We try to stick to a monthly budget,' Buzz said, 'and only use the money in the bank for big-ticket items. There's more than enough coming in through sponsors to cover our spending. We ask for Valentine's approval before buying big items. He comes along once a week or so to make sure everything is under control. He's a good guy for someone with such a soppy name.'

'What would you have me called?' Valentine asked. 'Dirk, Ironman, Storm?'

'Storm sounds good,' Buzz said, being immune to irony. 'Can we call you that from now on?'

'You might as well, as it's better than others you might use behind my back,' Valentine said.

'And what about you, Miss?' Buzz asked. 'Would you like a special name?'

'I think she's special enough as it is,' I said. 'Somehow Anji seems to suit her. Has a certain mystery about.'

'The mysterious Anji,' she said. 'Oooh! I like that. At least, Buzz, you didn't suggest Barbie. Get to know me more and I think you'll see that I'm not a Barbie girl.'

'I'll vouch for that,' I said.

Me, too,' said Storm. 'You should see her in motorcycle leathers.'

*Don't go there, Valentine,* I thought. You could affect these boys' lives forever.

'You make good coffee, Buzz,' I said.

'Really?' he said. 'Well, come down anytime for another.'

'How about girls?' Anji said. 'Does the system work for them as well as boys?'

'Yeah, you bet,' said Buzz. 'They're no different. Spend a bit more time on discussing make-up and girlie things, but we're all inclusive. We still insist any knives are handed in at the front door and they find that reassuring. No egos here are built by the size of your knife.'

'Anything else I should know?' I said. 'That I shouldn't need to know?'

'We're having a barbecue,' he said. 'A thank you to all our sponsors. One of our guys wants to be a chef. He's going to cook all the food. They'll be a non-alcoholic punch, in case you were worried about hordes of drunken guys terrorising the local neighbourhoods, and everything's recyclable. Say you'll come.'

'Put me down as a yes,' I said. 'I'll bring some friends, too.'

Providing I wasn't in prison.

CHAPTER NINETEEN

It was three o'clock on Friday afternoon and in two hours it would all be over. I would keep my bargain with Susan Blair and email my final report to the woman in charge at the NHS. Final, except for two murders unable to be solved. It would be a case of, 'Apart from that, Mrs Lincoln, how did you enjoy the play?'

It was probably the most unsatisfying job we had ever had. It was like a Greek tragedy. In Greek plays, the playwright would often not be able to think of an ending to tie up all the loose threads and leave the audience happy. There was always a solution, though. They sent the gods down from Olympus to sort everything out. It was called *deus ex machina*. The god from the machine. That was what I needed now.

Red was on duty, and I took him a coffee and stood by the hire car and chewed the fat. He was a Comanche and rightfully proud of his heritage. He had a farm in Texas that he had won in a poker game and said when it was all over, we should come and stay. He said that Texas had the best steaks in the world, and he would griddle some rib eyes. He'd become a mercenary when he didn't know what to do when his time in the army had come to an end. Johnny Silver had entered his life and it would never be the same again. If killing could be fun, he said, then that was the time to quit. There had to be a cause worthy to be fighting for. Some higher purpose. Something that made them stick by a moral code.

Red told me about some of the adventures he had had with Johnny and the crew Johnny had put together. There was an unbroken bond between them. They would die for each other. There is no higher praise than that.

We broke off our reminiscences on hearing a strange sound from inside. We rushed inside to investigate what it was.

Cherry was in the river room, bent double on one of the sofas. She breathed deeply between the groans.

'It's happening,' she said. 'It's happening. We need to go to the hospital before it's too late. Get my bag and let's go.'

Morag came in and I told her to call an ambulance. I sat next to Cherry and held her hand. I had no idea what else I could do to help her. I was powerless and didn't like that.

It took, thankfully, only ten minutes for the ambulance to come and I guided Cherry inside. I was about to climb in after her when the driver stopped me. It was against the rules. The best thing I could do, I was told, was to follow in the ambulance's slipstream to the hospital. I then did what was one of the most trusting things of my life: I threw Red the keys to the Beamer.

The ambulance was driving away as Red let in the clutch and pulled after it before I was fully inside. He caught up with the ambulance and we would be at the hospital in five minutes or so. Then came the red light. The ambulance made it through the traffic lights and we didn't. Red drummed his fingers against the steering wheel in frustration. After what seemed like an age, the light turned green and we sped away to the screech of burning tyres.

When we arrived at the hospital, I told Red to wait outside A&E while I checked the situation and worked out what he should do.

I ran inside and up to the reception desk.

'I'm looking for my wife, Cherry Shannon,' I said.

The lady on duty consulted her screen. 'I've no one of that name,' she said.

Maybe in the heat of the moment Cherry used her maiden name. Try Cherry Walker, please,' I said.

The woman looked at her screen.

'I see,' she said. 'She was tagged.'

What was going on? I was the one with the tag.

'What do you mean?' I said. 'Tagged?'

'She was diverted,' the woman said. 'There was a tag by her name: she was diverted to the Fairstead. You'll find her there.'

The Fairstead! I didn't know what was going on, but I didn't like it. The Fairstead was the last place I wanted her to be. I ran back outside and got in the Beamer. I took out my mobile and called Johnny.

'We have to work fast,' I said. 'They've got Cherry. We need to storm the place. You start and Red and I will join you.'

'What about your tag?'

'Sod the tag,' I said. 'There's no way I'm not going to be part of this. There's no time to lose. Pretty soon, I'll get a blackmail call. I'll stall. We need to take them by surprise. It's the only way. Check the operating theatres first and then the patient rooms if you hit a blank. Go, go, go!'

By a hairy drive, me clutching the handles in the car, we arrived at the hospital at the same time as Johnny and his crew. Stan handed Red and me a black hoody, face mask and plastic gloves. They were already kitted up. In we went.

'Over to you, Stan,' Johnny said.

'Pieter, take reception. No one comes in or out. Take out the telephone wires. No phone calls from now on.

'Red, line us up some transport that could cope with a stretcher. 'I'll take the first-floor rooms and confiscate mobiles.'

'Bull and Arthur, go to the operating theatres. Johnny and Nick, go through the patient room to see if Cherry is there and join up with us again at the operating theatres. Take any nurses to the operating theatres. Let's do it.'

We raced inside. The shock for the receptionist registered fear. Pieter said, 'Don't worry, we're not here to harm anybody. Pretty soon we'll be gone and things will go back to normal. Try not to scream or I'll gag you, and that won't be good. The only item I can get to gag you is my sock.'

Stan ran up the stairs; Bull and Arthur to the operating rooms. Johnny and I checked the patient rooms to see if Cherry was there and to take any mobiles. He took the odd-numbered rooms, and I took the even.

The level of fear among the patients was understandable. We tried to be as non-threatening as we could considering we were masked and hooded, but some of the patients screamed and reached for their call buttons, which would go unanswered. Whoever was tasked with that would have done his job. Stan would have covered that.

The first operating theatre was empty; the second was success.

Ferguson was gowned up. Cherry was lying on a stretcher and had no reaction to our entry, anaesthetised no doubt.

'Lay down the scalpel,' I said. 'We're taking Cherry. You have one phone call before we take your phone. Call your registrar and tell him we're coming and to be prepared for C-section.'

'What's the panic, Shannon?' Ferguson said. 'I'm only helping her. Don't you trust me? I suppose I could say things would be all right if you just sign that piece of paper before I start work. What do you say?'

'Bull, Arthur, grab him. Make sure he puts down the scalpel and makes the call.'

Ferguson dropped the scalpel and took out his mobile. He made the call. We were almost ready to go.

'Ever read *Of Mice and Men*?' said Bull to Arthur.

'Is that the one with Lenny?' said Arthur.

'You got it,' said Bull. 'Do you remember what Lenny did to Curly?'

'Yeah,' said Arthur. 'That was the best bit.'

'Let's have a race,' Bull said. 'First one to get a scream wins. You take left, I'll take the right. On your marks. Go!'

They each took hold of Ferguson's fists and started to crush the bones inside. As they squeezed, he sunk to the floor. He let out that final scream. He wouldn't be doing any operations for a long while.

'Let's call it a draw,' said Bull.

'An honourable draw,' said Arthur.

'One of you nurses comes with us to look after Cherry while we're travelling to the hospital. Who's best qualified?'

A tiny nurse nodded her head and we set off to take Cherry outside. We took the back exit and found Red waiting for us standing proudly by an ambulance. 'Will this do for transport?' he said.

Two ambulance men were seated propped up against a wall, gags in their mouths. Socks? Doesn't bear thinking about! Their hands were tied with telephone cables from an outside feed that Red had torn off.

'Play nicely, gentlemen, while we're gone,' Red said.

We loaded Cherry into the ambulance and I got inside with the nurse. Red got into the driving seat and found the controls. With lights flashing and sirens going, we were off.

Ferguson's registrar was waiting for us as we decanted Cherry inside the ambulance bay at the hospital. He whisked us off to a room that I guessed was improvised because there wasn't an operating theatre available. He gave me some scrubs, shoe coverings and gloves. I kitted myself up. The room had all manner of machines bleeping and stands and drips for infusions of whatever was needed. It, thankfully, was reassuring. Things were going to run like clockwork.

Red had followed us in and took charge of the tiny nurse to make sure there were no phone calls to raise an alarm.

I didn't know who the other people there were, but they seemed to know what they were doing. I took Cherry's hand and squeezed it for reassurance. For both of us.

The anaesthetist injected her with a local anaesthetic in preparation for what he said was called a spinal block where an injection was made into the area around the spinal cord. This meant she would be awake through the operation, but wouldn't feel anything below the waist. Sounded scary to me, but I wasn't the one having it.

'Just a moment now,' the doctor said, 'and everything will be numbed. Don't worry. This is quite a common procedure. I've done it many times.'

He picked up the scalpel and I looked away. I looked at Cherry and we locked eyes.

'You've changed,' she said. 'Your eyes. You've got that look now. Johnny's look. Eyes of steel. I'm going to have to watch you or you'll be gallivanting off to fight a war in some distant country as a mercenary. My god, I could murder a glass of chilled Chablis.'

There was the sound of a baby crying and I looked down to see the doctor pass a baby to a nurse.

'One down, one to go,' the doctor said.

He made it seem like it was some sort of production line, but maybe that was what it was for him.

A second cry sounded. Another bundle was handed to a second nurse.

'Just a bit of tidying up to do,' said the doctor.

I tried to not think of that.

'Congratulations,' he finally said. 'You have two healthy boys. We'll keep you in overnight, just as a precaution, and then you can go home.'

At last. The day had been successful. I was a father.

CHAPTER TWENTY

I phoned Norman, gave him the news and got him to keep his table reserved for seven people who had voracious appetites and heroic deeds to celebrate. It might be my last chance to have dinner outside the home for a while, too. On other occasions, where Cherry was fully functional, I would be looking after my wife and two bouncy boys. Frightening. Responsibility? Frightening, too. Maybe Cherry and I could celebrate through a Chinese takeaway and some experimental non-alcoholic white wine. No chilli, of course. Worth a shot, but I wasn't hopeful.

I heard the pop of a champagne cork when I entered our building. Valentine stepped into the hall from my office, where he had been watching out for me. There were plastic new-baby signs on the walls in the lobby — Morag? Beryl? All of them? We went through to the river room, where Norman was filling glasses of champagne for everybody.

There were hugs aplenty. Norman coughed to get every-one's attention.

'Who would have thought it?' he said. 'The great Shannon is a father. I would never have believed it. The days of self-indulgence — following any whim regardless of dan-ger — are over. I would guess the days of getting a good night's sleep are over, too. The days of putting himself up as bait are over, three. Let's drink to that. Let's drink to two healthy baby boys entering our family. I suspect are lives are changing, too, although I draw a line at nappy duty. Cheers.'

We toasted. We toasted till the third bottle had been emptied. I got myself ready for another celebration. Valentine said he would give me lifts there and back and I went upstairs to change for Toddy's. I looked around and visualised how the room could be sectioned off to give another bedroom so that the boys could have space of their own in the future. Why hadn't I thought of that sooner? I chose a pair of light blue chinos with a dark blue shirt, put on a suede bomber jacket that was old, but my favourite, and prepared to go downstairs. I thanked the gods for their protection. Many things could have robbed me of being here with two boys, the most beautiful wife in the world and a circle of true friends. It was written in the stars. Wasn't that what Cherry and I had agreed on? Don't be melancholy, Shannon, I chided myself. Take what the gods have given you and try to pay them back with every deed.

I went downstairs and Valentine and I got into his open-top Beetle. I'm not a good passenger, but Red was a whole new experience. I would never criticise any driver ever again.

Johnny and his crew were there when I arrived — Valentine being a safety-first driver, but I said I wouldn't criticise. There was one empty bottle of champagne in the silver bucket and two more being chilled beside it. Everybody got up and there were handshakes all around, plus a tearful hug from Arthur.

Toddy came up and gave me a smile.

'I know that many of you would normally go for steak, chips and salad, but how could I tempt you with this? I have two suckling pigs in the oven that have the best crackling in town. What about that?'

We nodded.

'I would think that a light starter would be appropriate,' Toddy said. 'How about some gravlax and mustard sauce or maybe a salad nicoise?'

179

'How about combining them on one plate?' I said.

'Can be arranged,' Toddy said.

He clapped his hands and a waiter brought over seven shot glasses and a frosted bottle of vodka. 'Norman said this was your favourite,' he said. 'It's Polish.'

'Ain't no other,' said Stan, picking up the bottle and filling our glasses.

Johnny held his glass in the air. 'Here's to a job well done and a celebration for the future. Cheers.'

We downed our glasses and Stan filled them up again. The vodka was good. No, it wasn't. It was great. The only drawback was it came in small bottles, but, knowing Toddy, there would be another bottle chilling somewhere.

Johnny made a speech, I made a speech, and pretty soon everyone had something to say.

'Where are you all going tomorrow?' I said.

'Back home,' Bull said. 'The first plane out of here back to our beautiful Caribbean island — Johnny to run his beach bar, and I'll be taking visitors game fishing. Normality will resume. The adventure has finished, and I'll miss it. Nice to get the adrenaline pumping again. It was good to meet you, Nick, and Arthur, too. Come and visit sometime.'

Stan was back to the hotel he ran, Pieter to South Africa as a game warden and Red to his ranch. I would be sad to see them go.

'Well, brother,' Johnny said. 'What do they say? It was good while it lasted, but you and I, Nick, have a future and a lot in the past to talk about. We'll get together when I'm next in London. Can't wait.'

The suckling pig arrived and looked perfect, just what you expected from Toddy. There was silence for a while. We were just finishing when we had an unexpected guest. Palmer.

A chair was instantly pulled up to the table as if by magic. Palmer leaned across before he sat down and shook my hand. 'Couldn't have happened to a nicer man,' he said. 'Who would have thought it?'

'People can't stop saying that,' I said. 'What's so incredible?'

'Because,' he said, 'life-changing things will happen that no one ever imagined. Take your Beamer. Soon you'll be driving a people carrier. *Brmm, brmm* out of the question. It's been good to know you, Nick.'

'Thank you, Dennis. That means a lot,' I said, losing the formality for a moment.

A waiter appeared and produced a glass. He placed it in front of Palmer and filled it with champagne.

Palmer took a sip and looked directly at me.

'Funny old day it's been,' he said. 'Something's been going on at a private hospital. I think, by coincidence, it's the one you've been working at. No one seemed to know what's been going on. A surgeon has two broken hands and doesn't seem to know how it happened. I suggested slipped on a bar of soap in the shower and he didn't seem to rule that out.'

'Any more detail?' I asked.

'Not clear,' he said. 'Something about a patient being abducted and, with all this, no one wants to press charges. Evidence? Nothing. No fingerprints apart from yours, but that's natural, seeing as you've been working there?' He took a sip of his champagne. Smiled. Eyed the Polish bottle wistfully. 'We could have made some sort of arrest, but there was little that can be done as far as evidence is concerned. Some idiot at the station wiped the CCTV pictures. And then the other thing is that your tag had been malfunctioning lately, so I had to turn it off and order a new one. Would you believe it, eh?'

'You're a good man, Dennis,' I said. 'How would being a godfather go down with you?'

'I'd be honoured,' he said. 'A perfect ending to a perfect day, apart from the murders, but you can't have everything, I suppose. We'll keep digging into it, but I'm not optimistic.'

'Never say never,' I said. '*Deus ex machina*. The gods will come down and sort it out.'

'Are you gentlemen here for business or pleasure?' Palmer said.

'Purely pleasure,' said Bull. 'Ain't no life outside of pleasure. Just a little something we had to do, but we don't count that as business. We were here for kicks. And we got 'em.'

'Haven't done a spreadsheet for a while,' Stan said. 'Nice to have a break in your lovely country. Got a good feeling inside.'

'I'm just a simple Comanche,' Red said. 'I go wherever Manitou chooses.'

'Me?' said Pieter. 'I'm back to preserving wildlife and stuff like that. Sometimes you have to make a judgement about what to save and what to cull. Satisfying when you get it right.'

'Have another drink, Dennis,' I said. 'I'll get Valentine to drive you home. Islington, isn't it? Red could get you there in five minutes, Valentine in twenty. I'd pick Valentine, if it was my choice.'

'It's a deal,' he said. 'I'll just call the missus and tell her not to set me out dinner. Meanwhile, another glass of that champagne would go down a treat and maybe a shot of that vodka, too.'

He got up from the table and found a quiet spot for his call. It was short, which I guessed was not a good sign. He came back and sat down. 'Apparently,' he said 'whatever she had cooked, I will have tomorrow, heated up in the microwave. Let's hope it wasn't salad.'

'You and Nick seem like an unlikely alliance,' Johnny said. 'What brought you together?'

'Like all things, life has a way of grabbing the foreseeable future and making it happen. God, what a pest he's been. The first one was a poisoning, the next was car bomb and that was followed by a brutal stabbing. It was all downhill from there.'

One of the black-and-whites came over with a menu and asked Palmer what he would like. There was one portion of suckling pig left. No contest. Whatever his wife had cooked that evening, it wouldn't be suckling pig. Make the most of it, Dennis.

'Shame we haven't been able to solve the murders,' Palmer said, 'but I guess you win some, you lose some.'

'If I can't win, I don't play,' said Arthur.

'You said it, bro,' said Bull. 'Took the words out of my mouth.'

'I've been reading up about you, Johnny,' Palmer said. 'Interesting story.'

'Got even more interesting these last few days,' Johnny said. 'Someone should write a book about it.'

'Maybe that should be me,' I said. 'If I ever get any free time in the future, that is.'

'Going to be some lonely nights ahead,' said Johnny. 'Use that time wisely. A story would be productive.'

And so I promised to write it. I even had a name. I would call it *Mercenary*.

# CHAPTER TWENTY-ONE

I took a couple of paracetamol the following morning and hoped no one would emit a loud noise. I dressed in a pair of black jeans and a gleaming white T-shirt that assaulted my eyes. I checked the babies' room and made sure everything would be perfect for their arrival home. I knew I would still be over the limit to drive, so asked Anji to do the honours. There were two large parcels in the hallway — two baby seats. Thoughtful and much appreciated. Something I should have thought of, but I was new to this baby game. Didn't know all the rules yet.

Anji dropped me off and left to find a parking spot — I would call her when we were outside and ready to leave. In the car, we talked of the way the Fates could rule your life, and the manner of her interview – changing clothes and identity half-way through. She laughed. 'How could I have done that?' she said. 'I didn't know I had it in me to pull it off.'

'Oh, you had it in you,' I said. 'First impressions count. There never was going to be anyone else who would be better to do the job. I think the Jewish word is chutzpah. Google it.'

'Does it hurt you not to have the Fairstead job resolved?' she said.

'I don't like unfinished business,' I said, 'but I'll have to push that out of my mind. There's more important things in life.'

'And life is important,' she said, 'and you have two more lives to think about now.'

'Do you know there's one of the things about the Fairstead job that irks me?' I said. 'I didn't manage to take that cosmetic surgeon Owen down a peg or two. Arrogance should be punished, and I wasn't able to do that. At least I scuppered their expansion plan, but it's a small consolation.'

We arrived at the hospital entrance and I got out. When I got to the ward Cherry was dressed and sitting in a high back chair with cots either side waiting for me. There was a bloom on her face that was a sign of the pride she felt inside. I bent down and kissed her on the cheek.

'What happened yesterday?' she said. 'It's all a bit of a blur after arriving at the Fairstead. One moment I was there, and the next I was here with you. I remember your eyes looking down at me. Something about them.'

'We had to persuade some people that you'd be better off here with Ferguson's registrar.'

'And how did you do that?' she said.

'We executed a plan,' I said.

'Do I want to know the plan and how you executed it?'

'Better not,' I said. 'Ignorance is bliss. There was one thing that will be amusing for you. Ferguson, somehow, managed to crush both hands and won't be operating for a long time. That was some recompense for unfinished business.'

'You and Palmer never managed to solve the murders?' she said. 'That's your unfinished business?'

'Palmer is philosophical about it,' I said. '"Win some, lose some" was his verdict. The police will still treat it as an open case, but it will move down the list and have less officers assigned to it. Palmer says that sometimes you have to take it on the chin, lick your wounds and get on with life.'

'Not something you're good at,' she said.

'No,' I said, 'but there's more important things to concentrate on. How are you feeling? Any hangover effects from the operation?'

'I'm as bright as a button,' she said. 'Couldn't feel anything else. Oh, aren't they beautiful?'

'Nothing better. Come on,' I said. 'I've had enough of hospitals to last me a lifetime.'

She stood up and we took one of the boys each and I wheeled the small suitcase out of the ward. Outside there was a wooden bench donated by a supporter of the hospital — his name on a little bronze plaque — Palmer. Interesting. Some ancestor? Maybe there was a story there.

We sat down and I called Anji. A minute or so later she pulled up and opened all the doors, put the suitcase in the boot and peered at the swaddled-up babies.

'Aren't they cute?' she said. 'Maybe you could let me hold one when we get back or even both. I'd be very careful, I promise.'

'It will be a pleasure,' Cherry said. 'I think we'll call you Auntie Anji.'

'Gosh, that makes me feel old. Stick to just Anji, please. Right, let's get in and be off.'

Cherry sat in the middle of the back seat with a baby in a seat carrier on each side. I climbed into the passenger seat and Anji slid into the driver's seat. We were off.

'Have you thought of names?' said Anji.

'We never talked about it. We didn't want to jinx anything,' I said. 'I would like their middle names to be Arthur and Norman.'

'Agreed,' said Cherry. 'Excellent. First names?'

'I thought of something heroic,' I said. 'Jason. You know the man who found the golden fleece to put everything right in the land?'

'Agreed again,' said Cherry. 'My choice now. I'd like it to be Edmond — you know, from *The Count of Monte Cristo*. The one who escaped from jail and put everything right. Well?'

'Agreed. Jason and Edmond it is,' I said. 'Perfect for the road to adventures.'

'How are you going to tell them apart?' said Anji.

'One — let's call him Jason with the middle name Arthur — has a small birthmark of the back of his neck that looks like a strawberry. To be on the safe side, we can also dress them in different colours, although Nick is a bit colour-blind.'

'For godparents I would like Palmer and Sir Gerald.'

'Agreed,' Cherry said. 'We need a female. I think Anji would be a delight.'

'Wow,' I said, 'We are thinking in tune today. It's been a very rewarding car journey.'

'One lesson to be learned is that we need a more practical car.'

I hated the word *practical*. It basically meant *dull*, but couldn't deny that the Beamer wasn't up to the job.

'You can keep the Beamer,' she said, as if she was inside my head. 'Tomorrow you can do some research and contact some dealers. The next time I go out, I want to do so in something designed for our needs.'

I nodded, although she probably didn't see it from the back seat.

When we arrived, Valentine came out to help, although I suspected he just couldn't wait any longer to see the twins. We went straight up to our floor and placed the babies in two cots wonderfully put together by Norman. They were blissfully asleep. Everyone followed us up and there were lots of *oohs* and *aahs* emitted. How great for them to grow up among such good friends. I made coffees for everyone and we willed the twins to wake, so they could be picked up and comforted.

Life was good — pretty much perfect — marred only by unresolved murders. That would have to be shrugged off and forgotten. Time to move on.

## THE END

# CHAPTER TWENTY-TWO

Or was it?

# CHAPTER TWENTY-THREE

'It's Prendergast,' the voice on the phone said. 'Michael Prendergast. You know, you came to see me after Cooper's death. It was a slow day today, no appointments, nothing urgent, so I thought I would look at the items we had stored relating to Fairstead, to see if anything could be binned as now irrelevant. There was a large envelope there. It said, "To be opened on my death", and was signed "Deborah Caxton". I don't know quite what to do with it.'

'I'll be there in an hour. Don't open it before I get there. Get some coffee brewing.'

I changed into a suit, put a bookmark at the place I was at in the accounts of our current job and leapt into the Beamer. I think I broke a speed record at some point — or some points, plural.

I was shown into Prendergast's office, where he sat deep in thought.

'This is all quite extraordinary,' he said. 'I'm worried about our vow to be a guardian, and the problems with discretion. Should I send it to next of kin, do you think?'

'Let's open it,' I said. 'Take a view when we see what is in there.'

I took a photo of the front and back of the envelope and reached for a letter opener on the desk. I took a breath and slid the knife across the top.

The contents were a bunch of manila folders. I opened the first and studied it. Then I called Palmer. 'I've got something you would die for. Be here as quickly as you can.'

I gave him the address and sat back in the client chair. 'Time for that coffee, Michael.'

While waiting for Palmer, I looked more deeply at the files. God, it all made sense now. Oh, this was going to be so sweet.

'This better be good,' Palmer said. 'I've dropped some urgent work to come out here.'

'This is better than good,' I said. 'This is to die for. Metaphorically speaking, obviously.'

'What have you got?' he said.

'I've got a bank robber for you, for starters.'

I slid one of the files across to him. He opened it and for a moment he was silent. He turned to me. 'Is this genuine?' he said. 'If it is, then it's dynamite. How did you come across this?'

'Mister Prendergast here found it in the storage facility for Fairstead. Insurance, I guess. I imagine there's work to be done for you, but when you've made some urgent calls, let's get everyone together and make some arrests.'

'Shannon, you're a marvel,' he said. 'So good I could kiss you. Metaphorically speaking, obviously. Let's do it. What a beauty!'

* * *

We drove back in convoy until I veered off to the office while Palmer went to the police station. I would wait for his phone call for a time, but our preferred slot was one o'clock when everyone should have a free hour. I sat down in the river room and made an espresso, while Anji and Valentine got ready to leave. They deserved to be in at the kill for all those days of sifting through the mind-numbing data.

When we got to Fairstead, we found Palmer there with two squad cars and a larger van, for taking suspects to jail. Four uniformed officers stretched their legs while waiting for the signal from Palmer. All of us entered the building and went to Cooper's office. The four uniformed officers stood by the windows and looked serious. Palmer, Anji and Valentine sat down at the conference table until the suspects were gathered. I paced around a lot.

Gordon Owen entered in shirt sleeves, his Rolex and gold cufflinks on show. 'I hope this isn't going to take long,' he said. 'I've got an operation scheduled for two o'clock.'

'You've no worries on time for a long while,' said Palmer. 'We'll take care of that.'

Susan Blair arrived next, black trouser suit, her red stilettos clacking on the wooden floor. She joined us at the table and looked nervous. She must have thought she had seen the last of us and here we were, back again.

Stuart Ferguson was the next arrival, his fingers poking out from two plaster casts. I tried not to give a smile, but failed. Barry Curnow, our man on hips and knees, came into the room in his beige suit and stared at the police officers. He sat down and looked at Palmer anxiously. The penny was dropping.

'Over to you, Shannon,' Palmer said.

'Let me tell you a story,' I said. 'Some of it is a bit hazy, but I'm sure you can help fill in the details. So, here we have, let's call him Mister A. Mister A is sitting there on his terrace outside his six-bedroom property on the Costa del Crime sipping a rum and Coke. He's bored, for one thing — misses the adrenaline of his previous days robbing banks. Wouldn't it be good to do one last job? He's also fed up with looking over his shoulder all the time. He needs another life. A false passport is easy to pick up if you have the money, of which he has got plenty. What he can't seem to overcome is his face. The moment he shows his face, then the police will catch him. There's so many arrest warrants against him, you could paper a large room.

'Then Mister A reads a story about a child suffering third-degree burns after a fire at her house. The little girl has a face reconstruction. She's unrecognisable after the operation. He has an idea. If they can do that for the little girl, surely they could work wonders for him? He reads on in the article and sees the name of the surgeon. Gordon Owen. One of only three in the country who can work such wonders. How am I doing so far, Gordon?'

'Rubbish,' Owen said. 'Utter nonsense. Where is your proof?'

'I'll come to that in due course, Owen,' I said. 'Meanwhile bear with me. Mister A gets risky. He's coming back to this country to talk to our resident cosmetic surgeon. To cross his palm with silver. Mister A also suggests a whole package deal — he says it would be even more of a deal if all the work from him — hip, knees, coloured contact lens, cataracts, gynaecological problems — could take place at the private hospital — family, friends, a few old lags. Referrals from him. Including overseas — people with funny names.

'Not just risky for Mister A, but for Owen, too. Owen has to discuss the idea with his fellow consultants. Maybe he goes down the pub or fixes an expensive restaurant. Maybe there's some cash sweetener on the table, eh, Owen? Owen starts with money. How much money could be coined in. It's a gamble. The other consultants and the financial director — Blair — would have to be cut in, as she will spot the change in his work patterns and could scupper the deal. Cooper won't spot it; he's too busy helping people. And there's his strong Christian ethic — he wouldn't contemplate such illegal happenings. The deal can't be cash: too much to put in the bank. Might arouse suspicion. The easiest way is to put the money into the business and take it out as dividends. It means Cooper will benefit, too, but it's not time for penny-pinching. Everyone agrees with the scheme — but only if there are equal shares. Rankles a bit, eh, Owen? Whatever. The scheme is set up and ready to go.'

Blair had her arms crossed defensively. Curnow leaned back in the chair and looked at the ceiling rather than look at me. There was a bead of perspiration on Owen's shaven head. Ferguson seeped vitriol at me.

'So everything is set,' I continued. 'Mister A gets his face reconstruction and his bright blue contact lenses, and the world is a better place. He's so pleased he mentions it to some people in the same line of business, including drug barons and some from eastern Europe, whatever . . . that's one of the bits that is hazy. Anyone want to help me out there?'

Silence.

'Fair enough. All goes swimmingly. Then Cooper spots something and digs around. Maybe the jump in revenue is too much. Someone catches on to what Cooper is doing. Blair, I suspect. She sees him checking back on the sales ledger. Cooper knows, it's clear, and just has to prove it before reporting to the police. This is a critical moment. Cooper must die.

'How did you decide which one of you to do the dirty deed?' I asked.

'He knows,' said Curnow. 'What's the point? We did scissors, paper, stone.'

It was time for me to sit back in my chair.

'You decided to kill a man with scissors, paper, stone. How little is one life in your scheme of things? Which of you was it?'

'It was me,' said Curnow.

'Watch what you say,' Owen said. 'They have no proof. Deny everything.'

'Can I cut a deal, DCI Palmer?' Curnow said. 'I reveal everything and get a shorter sentence?'

'I'll see what I can do,' said Palmer. 'No promises, but it will go in your favour.'

*Ooh, you little liar, Palmer.*

'It was easy,' said Curnow. 'I had a large paperweight on my desk. Just walked in the room. He was sitting at his desk. I walked behind him as if to look out of the window and then hit him on the head. Dragged him into his shower room. I'd already raided the drugs cupboard and taken the morphine and all the antidote of naloxone. I injected him five times. To make it look like suicide, I put the syringe into his hand.'

'His right hand,' I said. 'You'd worked with him all this time and didn't spot he was left-handed! Clumsy, Curnow. That was the first mistake.'

'Keep your mouth shut, Curnow,' said Owen. 'He can't prove anything. Don't dig in; you'll only make things worse for us. Hold your nerve.'

'Proof,' I said, 'the burden of proof, but let's move on to the second murder. Poor Caxton. She started to get cold feet. It had just become too much for her. She wanted out. She could spoil everything. She had to be eliminated. My guess goes something like this. You make sure she drinks a lot at the barbecue and has to use the bathroom. The downstairs toilet is in use — one of you sat inside there — another follows her upstairs. This suits her better, because she wants to check her make-up, put a bit more lipstick on. How's that going for a man uneducated in the esoteric world of make-up, Anji?'

'Spot on,' Anji said. 'You go up in my esteem.'

'So,' I said, 'one of you follows her up, and whack! Blow to the head to actually kill her, or maybe just stun — wine bottle, maybe, something else heavy you'd spotted on previous visits you'd made. Whatever. Break her neck for good measure. Fling her downstairs to make it look accidental. Who was it this time?'

'Me again,' said Curnow. 'I'd killed one person, so life couldn't get any worse for me.'

'Poor Debbie,' I said. 'She was so full of life. Just needed the right man to make everything perfect. You felt you were in the clear by giving each other an alibi.'

'Prove it,' said Owen.

'I promised you the proof a while ago now, so it's time for the big reveal.' I picked up the first file and slid across the desk to him. 'You see, Debbie felt uneasy from the word go. She took photos of before and after. Easy to hide a camera with all that equipment in her consulting room. Maybe she thought it would be like an insurance policy if something went wrong. Something with which she could do a deal with the likes of DCI Palmer. What do you think of that, Owen? Here resides Mister Freddie Ronson, bank robber extraordinaire. Except it wasn't Freddie Ronson any more. He's now Nigel Barnes, sales representative for a ladies' lingerie company. I blinded him years ago: Debbie managed to give back some sight, hence he could resume his former career. He needs to travel for his job. In and out of the country as many times as he likes. Progress on that, DCI Palmer?'

'Safely behind bars,' Palmer said. 'We've such a good case, he will be the one to cough.'

'By saying that he's the one to cough, DCI Palmer means everything. Everything done to Ronson. Everything about the men with dodgy pasts he has passed on to this hospital. Basically everything. Anything I have left out?'

Silence again.

'Take one look at your Rolex, Owen. Your cufflinks, too. If my memory serves me rightly, you're not allowed those in prison. Even if you were, they'd be the first thing you'd lose in prison. One last question,' I said. 'Was it all worth it?'

'I'll get you for this,' Owen said.

'But not for a long while,' I said. 'Over to you now, Chief Inspector Palmer. Let's lock 'em up.'

It seemed to take forever. Four people, multiple crimes — done this, accessory to that, the list went on. They were each cautioned, read their rights, handcuffed, and then led downstairs to the police van.

Anji and Valentine clapped.

'Pleased, Dennis?' I said.

'Would it be too cliched to say "over the moon"?'

'If it was,' I said, 'you'd be forgiven. I liked the handcuffs bit — much more dramatic than just leading them downstairs.'

'I thought so,' he said. 'Knew you'd appreciate that. We made simultaneous arrests across the country this morning, all easy to spot from the after photos in the files. I found my bank robber, Freddie Ronson.'

'I have history with him,' I said.

'So he said. Want to sit in for the interview for a gloat?'

'Wouldn't miss it for the world,' I said.

'Turned out nice again,' Palmer said. 'I think that's the phrase. Takes a lot to value you, Shannon, but when you do it's a hundred per cent. Absolute trust is a rare thing, but I trust you that much. Now, get out of my life before I get sentimental.'

He shook my hand, then gave me a hug.

'If you ever need me, I'm there for you,' he said.

'Well, executive and assistant no-job-title detectives, how did I do?'

'I think I can speak for Valentine,' said Anji, 'you're going to be insufferable. Let's hope it won't be for too long. Well done. I so love this job.'

And, so, the health of a hospital finished. Whether they found anyone to take it over, I didn't know, but suspected that I would become involved again in any rescue bid.

Valentine coughed to break my reverie.

'Yes, Valentine?'

'Don't you think we ought to get back?' he said. 'Jason and Edmond to check on. Lend a hand? That kind of stuff? That's as far as my knowledge goes.'

'OK, let's escape the chains of Fairstead and go to another world,' I said.

'Celebration tonight?' said Anji.

'Massive,' I said. 'Toddy's is out of the question. I'm not sure how Cherry would manage with the twins, but if we get the final clearance from her, it'll be a Chinese takeaway on our floor with hushed voices so as not to wake the twins. A job well done, all said and done. Thank you both. I couldn't have done it without you.'

And so, pleased as punch, we set off home. Would be good to get there. I was undecided about a decent cup of espresso or a large vodka and orange juice. Guess what I went for.

# EPILOGUE

*Silver can be more valuable than gold.*

Johnny and I sat in the executive lounge landside at Heathrow eating croissants and drinking espresso. His flight wouldn't board for another hour, but we wanted to spend as much time as possible together while he was in London.

'I was disowned by my family, you know?' he said. 'I took the rap for my younger brother Carlo for a loan that went belly-up. I then had no family. I didn't know what to do with myself. I decided to go back to my roots — your roots, too, now — and joined the Israeli army. They became my family. They taught me discipline, how to shoot an Uzi and to kill. Especially to kill. And I became very good at it.'

He broke off to take a bite of his croissant loaded with Little Scarlet strawberry jam — the best jam in the world. No expense spared in the executive lounge.

'When my time was finished in the army, I was at a loose end — back to no family again. I joined a team of mercenaries. I didn't like the way it was run. I wasn't alone. We decided to go freelance, and our group split off. You've met them now and can understand the strong bonds between us. We fought in various countries for regimes and businesses — a diamond mine, for example. We fought for the good and the bad, and didn't like the bad. We got to be choosy and whittled out the bad. We would fight for a cause we believed in and nothing else. But enough of me for a while. I want to know how you met Arthur — and Norman, who I haven't met yet. I want to know about prison and how you lost two fingers.'

'The fingers story can be told quickly; the rest will have to wait.' I took a sip of espresso and signalled the waiter for another round. 'I was in Brixton on remand while awaiting trial. It was like hell. I was put in a cell with Arthur. There was thug called Freddie Ronson. He was playing poker with Arthur, and Arthur was losing big time. He built up a big debt. I played in his place and took Ronson to the cleaners and wiped-out Arthur's debt and more. I cheated, of course, but Ronson could not prove it.'

The next round of espressos arrived and I took a sip. Good coffee.

'Ronson had it in for me after that and accosted me in the showers. He tried to rape me. I fought him off as best as I could, but it was a fight I was destined to lose. But Arthur had taught me to defend myself: fight dirty, he had said. As a way out from the attack by Ronson, I stuck two fingers into his eyes. These two fingers, the ones I have no more. I blinded him. On the night I was to move to Chelmsford, a lower category prison, two guards came into the cell — they had been bribed by Ronson. They put my two fingers into the steel door and slammed it shut. I've not been good with closed doors and spaces since.'

Johnny looked at his watch. 'Time to board,' he said. 'We have many tales to tell. I want to hear more. When I'm next in London, let's eat together at Toddy's.'

'Sounds good,' I said. 'I have to discover my past. To catch up on a new family.'

'And don't do anything stupid. I want you here in one piece when we next meet. I must go. Give me a hug, brother.'

And I did.

* * *

198

The twins were six months old and beginning to take on individual personalities. They both liked to smile when I read their bedtime stories. They laughed at the funny voices I put on, but Cherry said it was just wind. Oh, ye of little faith.

Jason liked to be quiet, while Edmond preferred everything busy around him. Edmond always woke before Jason who would quite easily have slept on if it were not for his brother's cries.

I wondered whether I was like Jason while Edmond had the buccaneering spirit of Johnny. Two souls united in blood. Let them never be apart.

I felt that while I was in prison I had found myself, but the discovery that Johnny was my brother had thrown everything back in the mix. I had to re-evaluate myself again. The parents that I thought of as my parents were no longer so. The sister that I thought of as my sister was no longer so. Would it have been different if I had known the truth? No. Fate would have blown me on to this point. It had to be. Could I imagine another world without Cherry and the twins, without an Arthur and a Norman in my life? No.

Johnny and I slotted into a pattern. Whenever he was in London, we would have dinner at Toddy's and spend those few hours talking of histories. On one occasion, he had brought along some photos of Mother and his brothers Roberto and Carlo. Roberto, the elder brother, was scowling in each photo; Carlo, the younger, smiling and showing his expensive dental work.

I reciprocated and showed him pictures from my childhood and as a young man, many with my sister. He said it was the butterfly effect: how one trivial event — my sister walking along a quiet road — can change a life forever.

Johnny came to visit us at the wharf and met Cherry and the twins and the rest of the crew. Valentine was in total awe as he listened to some of Johnny's adventures. Anji just stared, speechless — a little younger, and she would have asked for a photo of him to pin up on her wall. Maybe she would in any case.

The business was at a new high through the publicity around videos posted by Buzz and others. We would need Cherry to be functioning soon, but that had to wait till the twins had developed a regular routine and life was more predictable.

Life was as perfect as it could have been, except for one thing. Hanging over my head like the sword of Damocles, was the trial. Time ticked relentlessly on and was running out with each day.

'In case I forget,' Cherry said, 'good luck tomorrow.'

'Keep your fingers crossed for me. I may need all the help I can get. If you see any black cats around, let me know.

* * *

*Shannon's trial*

'Shannon is infuriating, My Lord,' Palmer said, addressing the judge from the witness box. 'He likes to play the fool. He asks stupid questions to try to winkle out the truth. He challenges people by appearing dumb, so that their defences are down. By doing so, he gets people talking and saying too much. It's a rare gift. He gets more from an interrogation than I, a seasoned police officer, could ever get.'

We were in the Old Bailey, the central criminal court of England and Wales, with its figure of a woman on top of the dome holding a sword in one hand and the scales of justice in the other. Against common perception, there was no blindfold. No blind justice. It was the closing day of my trial, and Palmer had the jury enrapt. The verdict would obviously be guilty — I had pleaded to that and there was indisputable evidence of the crime through a video taken at the scene that had gone viral. It was all about the sentence — whether I finished up back in prison where I had once spent seven years of my life. Everything depended on today. My wife, children, business, all in balance on those scales. Which way would it tip?

'My Lord,' Palmer continued. He stood straight-backed, looking as immaculate as ever. He cut a solid picture in his plain grey suit and brilliant white shirt. He looked like a person to believe in. That was the point of calling him as a witness for the defence. 'Shannon likes to take on the role of wise guy, as if he takes nothing seriously. Like it's all a game and he is one of the lowly pawns. At some times, that pawn advances to become a queen, the highest piece on the chess board. He is exasperating and raises your blood pressure. It can be easy to lose your temper with him. I have done so at times in the past. All of which I regret.'

Palmer paused to take a sip of water to lubricate his mouth — hands sweat, mouth dry … isn't that what they said in *The Magnificent Seven*?

'He makes decisions on trust rather than logic,' Palmer said. 'If Shannon believes in someone, he will fight for them with his life. He never abandons someone or passes the buck or turns his back. He can be your truest friend and advocate.

'Shannon is a fighter for justice. He often likes to deliver that justice himself, one of the reasons why we are here today. He is cool, calm and collected. Mainly. I had never seen him act irrationally before that fateful day. An aberration while under shocking pressure from a heart that had seen his wife shot by an arrow. Surely, he can be forgiven for a moment of madness when heart overruled head.

'Shannon has helped catch murderers, drug lords, money launderers and people traffickers. Without that help, these people would have escaped scot-free to continue their crimes against society.'

'To sum up, Chief Inspector,' my barrister said, 'what would the world be without Shannon?'

'A darker place,' said Palmer. 'No question.'

'You may stand down,' my barrister said. 'I call now on Brian Thomas,'

It took a while for the next witness to understand his full name — no one used it. He was just Buzz.

'How old are you?' the judge said, when Buzz was in the witness box.

'Fourteen, sir,' he said. 'Sorry, Your Honour.' He looked ill at ease — in a suit and tie. Chang's?

'And you are happy to give evidence?' the judge said.

'Yes, Your Honour,' Buzz said. 'Anything to help Mister Shannon.'

'Tell the court your story,' my barrister said.

'It was a chance meeting,' Buzz said. 'I was a part of a gang mooching around looking to steal some things to sell — hubcaps are easy, but anything would do. Mister Shannon wanted to see where the rest of the gang was. He gave us a talk about the dangers of carrying knives. He got a friend of his — Arthur "Dangerous" Duggan — to teach us self-defence. I could tell Mister Shannon didn't like us lounging away on a stretch of concrete all day. Mister Shannon got us a place to meet so we were off the streets — I'd never really had a place to sit and think about my life — but now there was a place to shelter. He taught us about honour: a moral code, he said. He taught about respect for people. He taught us about right and wrong. Without Mister Shannon, I'd still be looking for anything to steal and sell. Without Mister Shannon, I could have stabbed someone over some petty gang violation. I could be up for a murder charge. The rest of the story you would have seen. Mister Shannon is my role model. I wouldn't be here today without him. I'd be in prison. Now or eventually. He deserves a chance. He gave us, and kids like us across the country, a chance. We should return that favour. I love him, Your Honour. He changed my life.'

'No more witnesses, Your Honour,' my barrister said. 'I will now sum up on the case against the defendant.'

The jury retired to give their only possible verdict. There was nothing more to do.

It took longer than expected. Open-and-shut case. What was the problem? If I had been a smoker, I would have had three by now. Martin, my solicitor, shrugged his shoulders, signalling that he didn't understand.

'Have you reached a verdict?' said the judge when the jury returned. 'How do you find the defendant?'

'Guilty,' said the foreman of the jury. 'But there is one more thing. We consider the defendant acted with diminished responsibility through what had happened to his wife of just minutes on their wedding day.'

The foreman sat back down.

'It is not your remit,' said the judge, 'to consider such things. That is my duty only.'

Martin crossed his fingers.

The judge summed up the case. Easy thing to do.

'We cannot have people taking the law in their own hands. We cannot have a vigilante society. I have no option but to impose a custodial sentence.'

My heart sank. Custodial sentence. Prison.

'I sentence you to two years in prison,' the judge said.

There was still a chance. Slim, but a chance nonetheless.

'Suspended,' said the judge, 'in view of diminished responsibility.'

Martin punched the air. My barrister frowned at such an outburst, but shook my hand in a pumping hold and smiled. 'Don't ever do anything like that again, Shannon,' the barrister said. 'Much as I value the fee I would earn. Palmer appealed to the jury's head, Buzz to its heart. You should be eternally grateful to that lad. Now be gone with you. Time to answer questions from the press. Whatever "viral" means, I think you will become so again.'

Martin gave me a hug. 'God, you were so lucky,' he said. 'It could easily have gone the other way. The fact there was premeditation was sticky. There was the day's gap between the attack on Cherry. That made the idea of diminished responsibility a little tricky. Like the man said, and to paraphrase, don't do anything so stupid again.'

A baby cried.

'Your fan club is waiting to speak to you,' Martin said. 'Good luck, Nick. I hope not to have to see you, again.'

Palmer and Buzz were waiting for me. I hugged them both. Buzz had tears in his eyes.

'What can I say?' I said. 'I will forever be in your debt for what you said today.'

'I'd like that in writing,' said Palmer. 'I'll remind you of that the next time I need a favour.'

'Come and have a coffee the next time you're passing,' said Buzz. 'We're getting a proper machine with pods and everything, just as you like.'

'Like with Palmer,' I said,' if ever you need a favour or if you ever need a friend, I'm here for you. When you get that machine, let me know and we'll plan a reunion. Arthur, Valentine and Anji will come. Maybe Norman, too, if there's a need to run through events on the charity he set up for you. See you soon, Buzz.'

The viewing gallery emptied and I could see everyone coming down the stairs. Cherry had Edmond and Beryl was carrying Jason. Anji, Valentine, Arthur and Morag were all there.

Then it struck me.

'Where's Norman?' I said.

'We left him in charge,' Morag said.

'Goodness knows what trouble we'll be in when we get back,' I said.

And I was right.

**THE END**

# THE JOFFE BOOKS STORY

We began in 2014 when Jasper agreed to publish his mum's much-rejected romance novel and it became a bestseller.

Since then we've grown into the largest independent publisher in the UK. We're extremely proud to publish some of the very best writers in the world, including Joy Ellis, Faith Martin, Caro Ramsay, Helen Forrester, Simon Brett and Robert Goddard. Everyone at Joffe Books loves reading and we never forget that it all begins with the magic of an author telling a story.

We are proud to publish talented first-time authors, as well as established writers whose books we love introducing to a new generation of readers.

We have been shortlisted for Independent Publisher of the Year at the British Book Awards three times, in 2020, 2021 and 2022, and for the Diversity and Inclusivity Award at the Independent Publishing Awards in 2022.

We built this company with your help, and we love to hear from you, so please email us about absolutely anything bookish at feedback@joffebooks.com.

If you want to receive free books every Friday and hear about all our new releases, join our mailing list: www.joffebooks.com/contact.

And when you tell your friends about us, just remember: it's pronounced Joffe as in coffee or toffee!